THE ARSONIST'S SONG
HAS NOTHING TO DO WITH FIRE

THE ARSONIST'S SONG
HAS NOTHING TO DO WITH FIRE

A NOVEL

Allison Titus

etruscan press

Etruscan Press
Wilkes University
84 West South Street
Wilkes-Barre, PA 18766
(570) 408-4546

WILKES UNIVERSITY

www.etruscanpress.org

Published 2014 by Etruscan Press
Printed in the United States of America
Cover and interior design and typesetting by Julianne Popovec
The text of this book is set in Goudy Old Style.

First Edition

14 15 16 17 18 5 4 3 2 1

Library of Congress Cataloging-in-Publication Data

Titus, Allison, 1976-
  The arsonist's song has nothing to do with fire : a novel by / Allison Titus.
    pages cm.
  Summary: "The Doctor was looking for the blueprint. Drawer after drawer he lumbered his way around the office, a map of the ribcage in his head. Last night he'd dreamed the wings again and the dream gave him an idea. More of the rib, dismantled, would make the wing frame more flexible.In The Arsonist's Song Has Nothing to Do with Fire, Vivian Foster connects with an arsonist and a radical plastic surgeon whose mission is to build human wings.Allison Titus lives in Virginia with poet, Joshua Poteat, and their four dogs. She has also written a book of poetry"~ Provided by publisher.
  ISBN 978-0-9886922-5-1 (pbk.)
  1. Loneliness~Fiction. 2. Arsonists~Fiction. 3. Plastic surgeons~Fiction. 4. Friendship-
-Fiction. 5. Psychological fiction. I. Title.
  PS3620.I87A89 2014
  813'.6~dc23
                              2013046182

Please turn to the back of this book for a list of the sustaining funders of Etruscan Press.

To my family.

& to JP.

Sometimes people die trying to do things.
That's OK.
There are things more important
than life or death.

—Mary Ruefle, "Elegy for a Game"

ACKNOWLEDGMENTS

With infinite gratitude to the National Endowment for the Arts for a literature fellowship and the time it provided.

Thank you: to the editors of *Ninth Letter* and *Verse* magazine for publishing early excerpts from this manuscript. To my friends, some of whom were early readers, some of whom read multiple drafts, all of whom were endlessly supportive: Marie Potoczny, Paige Ackerson-Kiely, Meg Rains, Rob Schlegel, Barbara Yien, Brian Henry, Josh Harmon, Katy Resch, Kelly Kerney, Ann Marshall, Alanna Ramirez, Jenny Koster, Tom de Haven.

Thank you to the mongrels of my heart who kept me company for the many years that I wrote this: Ruben, Piper, Elly, Daisy.

And most of all, to JP: for every single thing.

THE ARSONIST'S SONG
HAS NOTHING TO DO WITH FIRE

On the morning of the day she died, Vivian Foster woke earlier than usual, woke to dim half-light, slung down clouds fat with impending rain, the shrieking pushcart sounds of the limping bottle collector, the pigeons' scuffed purrs rummaged up from the alley. *She is survived by* was where she faltered, no heir, no indebted, no lover to claim—but she thought her obituary through every night anyway. Worried over all the mechanics of the evered this and evered that. A bad habit. The bargain for a last resort: If all else failed/If it couldn't get any worse. Sometimes the death she imagined was uneventful: she grew old and died in her sleep. More often, though, an elevator collapsed on its cable at the fifty-third floor; or the train derailed; or the gas pump, struck by lightning, went up in flames. Vivian was convinced a freak accident would befall her eventually, some pathetic and arbitrary devastation. So she resigned. She waited for the appropriate disaster.

In the meantime, she practiced dying, submitting to the idea of death in all its terrible versions. Car accident, factory fire, heart attack; hypothermia, avalanche, homicide; tuberculosis, malaria, syphilis: steady and progressive illness was, by far, the worst. The body wasted to its husk of bone; the drafty sick room with its thin-sheeted bed; limp wrist pale and buckled on the fleece. Guessing at every potential cruelty or misfortune was tedious, for sure, was oppressive, but she couldn't quit. She had to practice dying, and practice dying, and remain vigilant by practice-dying. And so on.

The wafers were arranged like pocketknives on the heirloom doily and delivered, as was customary, at tea. Little did Viv know the cakes were laced with arsenic. That one mouthful would loiter, hot, at her throat. By the time the fever tucked into her lungs, a small fire, it was too late to remedy the oversight. The assistant would be stripped of his badge and escorted from the building, but not before Vivian died. The doily was woven from horsehair and patches of Spanish moss tugged from oaks shading the town's cul-de-sacs and cemeteries and parks. When the assistant used the doily to mop urgent and rough at Vivian's face, small scratch marks hatched pink across her pale skin, there and there and there.

The cab was gone by the time Viv reached the front door; she should've asked the driver to wait—who knew how this would go, she thought, looking up and down the street. Large yards flocked large houses; long driveways held surplus cars. It was hardly September, but the neighbors had installed a fiberglass deer mid-prance in their hedge. She counted to fifty by twos and rang again, and this time the door opened and a woman leaned out, squinting around in surveillance. The woman's face was the wide, blank hull of a ship frantic for mooring, her eyes prodded by dark pockets of no good sleep.

"I'm Vivian," she said, in case the woman didn't remember. "You're—"

"Helen, of course, of course," the woman said. "Come in."

Vivian followed her down the shotgun hall to a dining room where Helen refilled her glass, and asked Vivian if she'd like a drink and, if so, would she get another glass from the kitchen.

"Upstairs, straight back, top shelf over the stove, you can't miss it," she said.

Vivian started up the stairs, wondering what she'd gotten herself into. She'd found the ad in the classifieds, where would-be brides auctioned off their dresses like new. And here she was, because somehow, she'd allowed herself to come all this way—eight hours by train, out of the station before sunup only to break down near Nashville; coffee machine out of order; a lukewarm beer and stale sandwich for lunch; piles of cattle out the window, laundry lines flagged with shirts; then, closer to the city, the junkyards, the underpasses tagged with names like Retro Fit and Halo—without knowing what was going on.

The stove gleamed silver and untouched and the refrigerator shined blank, no postcards under magnets. A bowl in the sink. She stalled in the kitchen for a few minutes, the first pulse of dread swelling up, thinking what was she doing there, why had she come—

For a few minutes she just stood there, admiring the bell white geometry of the floor tiles and taking down a glass.

Vivian lived in strangers' houses. The way some people are nurses. Or chefs. The way a nurse catalogues injuries and reads fevers, and the person in charge of the kitchen paces the stations shouting BLACKEN THE OYSTERS and ORDER UP. Taking up in strangers' houses was just something she did, until by default it became her occupation. It suited her—she preferred departures to abiding. She preferred elsewhere over everywhere else. She enjoyed how noncommittal her existence seemed, how theoretical. Letters took months to reach her through the limbo of forwarding last known address to last known address. A locker at the Lost Mail Repository in St. Paul or Cleveland held old packages, bills, wedding announcements, et cetera, that never found her, all those obligations gone missing, and when she thought about that she felt relieved. Off the hook. Which made her the opposite of a nurse. She was not one to oversee anyone's bedside. She did not dote. And when you got down to it, anyway, her life depended on solitude and the extended absences of other people. If no one ever left, she'd have no place to go, and she knew what to expect from these temp arrangements—hot water, a decent couch, someone else's weather and fingerprints; someone else's dust.

That first night she learned everything. Helen at the other end of the table, about to cry or beyond crying; the muscles in the face going the same either way, tensing then wilted. Vivian concentrated on the window just behind Helen. When the wind picked up, drooping branches gusted against the side of the house, tapped the glass.

"My husband's gone," Helen said, cradling her head with one hand like a headache. "Paul, goddamn it—he's just, how do you—" She stopped to take a drink and shrugged.

Vivian tried to keep her face regular, tried to not look alarmed— though she was alarmed—because looking alarmed wasn't going to help Helen, who was telling her how Paul didn't come home from his office one night, where he still went twice a week even though that semester he was on sabbatical. How he was studying a certain kestrel of a certain northern region of some habitat off the Indian Ocean.

She said, "It wasn't someone else, if you're thinking that. We weren't having trouble. The police ask about my marriage every other day, there's nothing I haven't answered twice already. It's fucking humiliating. We were leaving that morning, the next morning, for Montserrat."

Vivian pictured Montserrat: volcanoes. Currents like harp necks. Then sat there because what could she say, everything had changed. Now a man was missing. But she had no history here, no way to tabulate differences—see, that chair's his favorite and the cat won't budge.

"It's been a month," Helen said. "A month and two days."

So she was going to Florida where her sister lived. Pensacola for the time being.

"And you will take care of this," she said.

The table, the unopened mail, the empty bottle, the empty house. Said it with a casual sweep that included every forty-watt in every fixture, every chore, every joke souvenir from every pseudo-historical day trip they'd taken.

"You're a saint for coming," she said, "A saint." She repeated it under her breath; she repeated it to the ceiling, her head swayed all the way back. She was drunk.

Vivian tried not to picture the chair tipping back, the crash of Helen breaking her head open, how she'd have to call an ambulance because she couldn't drive stick. Vivian wasn't a saint. Paul's vanishing, which she could never tell Helen, meant she'd have a place to stay a few more weeks. If he returned tomorrow she'd be disappointed, not to mention homeless. Nothing about what she was doing there made her anything more than a short-term contract employee. There wasn't even a dog to require walks and feedings and fresh bowls of water.

After some time had passed Vivian said, "Do you have any idea where he might be?"

Helen sat up in her chair then leaned forward, possibly surprised, Vivian thought, to realize she wasn't alone in the room.

"I'll tell you who doesn't have a fucking idea, not a fucking clue," she said. "Jenner and that idiot Maxwell—they made me wait a week to file the report when it was obvious the third night he was missing. They keep showing up with questions and the one with the mustache refuses to tell me a thing, he can't tell me anything."

She set the bottle down clumsy. "Like I'm just in the goddamn way," she said.

"No, I don't know where he is. It's bullshit, it doesn't make sense."

Helen reached into the jacket draped over her chair.

"Do you mind?" She held up a sad looking pack of cigarettes, dumped the last three out on the table. "Want one?"

Vivian shook her head.

Helen smoked for a minute while Vivian tried to come up with something to say.

"They're Paul's," Helen said, watching the cigarette between her fingers.

"He's supposed to quit."

Much later Vivian stared at the guest room ceiling, thinking about it. If she died in this city, it would be from drowning. Helen's house wasn't far from the lake and Vivian couldn't swim. Late November afternoons always turned colder and darker faster than you expected. It would be tragic, sure, but barely publicized, because around here the half-hearted gang-crime dominated local news. She closed her eyes, held her breath and tried to imagine it. The pitch black, the thick water that pulled through her clothes, pummeled her arms her legs her face and burned sharp as it flooded her nose, mouth, throat, lungs—she'd choke hard before blacking out, which she knew would be painful but she wasn't sure how, exactly; would she pass out before or after she felt her legs go numb, before or after her arms grew too heavy to lift. The cause of death would be logged in some med. tech.'s chart as *Asphyxiation*, not suffocation, but that's all drowning was, a suffocation. What bothered her was how long it would take, would it be minutes or hours? How long would she drift like that in the water, jetsam? She would have to research death by drowning.

Then she remembered. And how did she forget, anyway. How did she lose track of the particulars enough to forget and then be reminded. Except how your hand forgets skin and skin forgets muscle. How it all just endured in the meantime, three entire days passed and she hadn't called. It didn't matter. Maybe her mother answered and she was still alive out there, in whatever that Nebraskan ghost town was, that shelf of dust where her trailer was slung. But maybe she didn't answer, twelve rings nothing, twenty rings nothing, because maybe she was dead. There was no way to know whether she was dead or not, unless at some point she answered. In a few days, a week, two weeks. So Vivian called and called and hung up on her mother. They hadn't spoken since her mother left North Carolina for Nebraska's broken radios and half-empty storefronts, maybe six, maybe seven years ago. She pictured her mother pacing back and forth in a barely-heated trailer. Hinged on an overgrown lot. A trailer with carpet and walls dingy like dredged up oyster casings. The squawk of her pet bird, Picnic, if Picnic was still around. A loud television.

Three days had passed and she hadn't called. Her mother wouldn't notice. She didn't remember Vivian, Vivian's brother (Seth), or what century was dawning (it was 1989). But unless she called and hung up, Vivian couldn't stop thinking through the desperate scenarios. A broken wheelchair; rats in the kitchen; a man with a rifle pounding through the trailer door with the blunt of it. She felt guilty, thinking about her mother alone, out in the middle of nowhere, even if she'd chosen exile. That almost made it worse.

Vivian sneaked out of her room, skirted the kitchen, and ducked into the office. She closed the door until it was almost flush with the threshold but not caught; a strand of light fell through from the hallway. The phone was an old cordless and dull static buzzed through the reception. She punched in the numbers and waited. She could make out some books on the shelf above the desk, mostly unfamiliar birds and geographies. *Birds of the West Indies* by Houser. Three rings, four rings. *White-Bellied Emeralds and Red-Legged Honeycreepers of Belem*. Six rings. All those wires traipsing the skies from anywhere to anywhere else, crossing fields, eight rings, and highways and irrigation canals and rivers and mountain ranges and deserts and parking lots and glaciers, erected, nine rings, against great spaces in hopes of a voice on the other end, signals and waves arranged into a recognizable pattern.

"Hello," the voice insisted, "hello, hello, who—"

Vivian hung up. She could never bring herself to say anything. And what was there to say? She couldn't bear to introduce herself.

As she slipped back down the hall, she looked over at the stairs, down to where they curved to the foyer, and hesitated. Helen was down there, sitting on the bottom step, her forehead bent to her knees. Vivian watched, kind of frozen in place. Grief was a thing that filled every air sac of your kidney-shaped lungs but all it left you with was a hollow, defeated posture, kind of a weakness at the ribcage. To ache for someone, every brutal hour with no news—Vivian would rather be the one who was lost, distracted by efforts to get found, not the one back home, left to deconstruct conspiracies and post fliers. As she stood there, she realized Helen was crying. First her shoulders then her whole tucked-over body shuddered. Embarrassed to see her like that, to think that Helen could know she'd seen her like that—crumpled up, a little out of control—Vivian held her breath as she crept back to her room, careful not to make any noise. She closed her eyes and pretended to sleep and practiced drowning.

Helen was still drinking when she left the next morning, quick sips from a mug that said SAVE A MANATEE on one side and COW OF THE SEA on the other above a manatee face. Vivian helped her to the cab with her bags, shoving them into the backseat while Helen repeated last-minute reminders. Emergency phone numbers, spare keys, instructions for the mail. Vivian watched the taxi as it disappeared down the street. And then, as per usual, she was alone with what she had temporarily inherited.

Ronny Stoger was not a career man nor a tradesman nor a man with management potential, per se. Ronny was a peddler. He worked at the quarry off Graverton is what he'd tell anyone who asked. Meaning he worked at the gift shop and junkyard adjacent the quarry, Concrete Jungle, a place that salvaged claw foot tubs, pinewood church pews and broken desks, but specialized in the sale of concrete squirrels and deer meant for gardens. For example, concrete birdbaths, concrete pigeons. Concrete giraffes, rabbits, monkeys. The whole lot was bland, stationary, stony—of course. But the stillness bothered Ronny some days more than others. Why domesticate cement?

The town Ronny lived in was a town of lesser-known fast food restaurants and colored glass repositories. There was a minor college, and for those kids there wasn't much more than the pool hall, which had two pool tables, a mechanical bull that was mostly out of order, and dollar pitchers after eight. There was an old movie theatre downtown, a dry cleaners, a post office. Must be more, but that seemed like most of it as far as Ronny could tell—not much had changed. He'd been back at his father's house for almost three months, out of juvie, done with service hours. Anyhow, his mother wanted him out, not stuck there after everything. Because Ronny set fires. Small fires, sure, but left to their own devices—caught on the wind, for example—small fires might forge a remarkable blaze.

On days this foggy, the quarry disappeared. The clouds filled in the gap so you could walk right up to the edge before you realized you were standing over the pit, a 250-, 300-foot drop. Days like this no one came around. The camps got off for zero visibility but Ronny still had to man the yard till dusk. He brought in six-packs to pass the time; he propped his feet on the desk, leaned his head back against the wall, thought about how he was too old for this. Most everyone he'd known was out of Central by now, if they'd gone, or done with hair dresser school or auto repair or refrigeration or funeral services training. Whatever people did, they were doing it. Cutting hair, fixing cars, pressing shirts for dead bodies.

This line of thinking got him restless. What the men at the quarry did was actual work, work that required safety gear and callused hands. He knew because the foreman owned this place too and he stopped in sometimes near end of day, with his hardhat and vest and roughed up grip.

Ronny stood, finished his beer and lined it up with the other cans on the desk. The office was too small to pace. He half-kicked the trash bin, toed it to the wall. He pulled at the dime store bell yarned to the door handle that rang for customers. He looked out and made sure. No customers. He pulled at the filing cabinet drawers for no reason. They were rusted and shrieked open to reveal office supplies mostly, envelopes, old paperwork. In the third drawer down he found the bank deposit bag, right there on top, bingo. His boss hadn't turned it in. He unzipped it, it was pretty slim, pulled out a bill without looking, slipped it in his back pocket. Not a big deal but his heart beat faster, slightly, because it was an asshole thing to do, to steal from your boss for no reason except you were shitty bored. He sat back down at the desk and opened another beer.

It started with an average procedure. Vivian had a French professor and the French professor had a sister; the sister was having throat surgery and would be a l'hopital pour une semaine. Vivian had an ear for almost silent endings. A week became a month. A minor complication; another surgery. The month lingered. Vivian tried not to think of the body and all its soft organs but she did what she could: watered the plants, sorted bills, fed the fish. House one: single-family condo, well maintained.

Posted at the local video rental place was a flier: parents seeking a house sitter while they moved their son out west, References From The College Required. The Douglas family—dried eucalyptus wreaths on every window, a damp basement, a freezer full of low-sodium TV dinners. Vivian watched game show reruns and flipped through albums of old family photographs, page after page of weddings and birthdays. Yellow dresses, yellow cakes. House two: split-level, two-bedroom, detached garage.

One week in July: a friend of a friend's cousin, just married. The newlyweds were going on holiday and Vivian had nowhere else to be. She took in the paper, smuggled whiskey from the bar. The cousin's name was Kitty. Music from the strip mall's Mexican restaurant accessorized the neighborhood all night, like colored lights strung on Christmas trees—tinny and cheerful and relentless. House three: suburban ranch, wall-to-wall carpet, beige.

House after house after apartment. Bedrooms and kitchens and back doors and deadbolts. How similar they became, all the different rooms in all the different towns, each one as familiar as it was strange. Every oversized breadbox. Every welcome mat. All the guitar cases in all the closets stashing ordinary porn.

When she ran out of houses, the worst were nights spent in the bus station, so when it came down to that, she did what she could. And breaking in was easy. Mail piled up near the door, lights automatic at dusk, curtains never drawn—chances were the house was empty. She cased neighborhoods that way, kept track of where she might go next, religiously considered her alternatives.

This was how people lived: they left keys under their flowerpots, taped them inside their mailboxes, snapped magnetic boxes inside the wheel wells of their cars. They left windows unlocked like they were leaving instructions. *Here, the bar's not soldered. Slide it out and the window practically opens itself. Here, the deadbolt sticks so be sure to pull forward then turn.*

The first time, it was winter. The back door was unlocked; she held her breath and counted by twos to a hundred, a nervous habit. She stayed three days. Slept on the couch, left the lights off in the afternoon, drank water straight from the tap. She took a Polaroid of the kitchen: a sick argyle of green and yellow tiles, rotting pears on the table. She couldn't say she wasn't nervous. The second time was a year later. An ex-boyfriend's house. She meant to stay for the entire Memorial Day weekend. The family had a wedding to attend in Connecticut; Vivian had backed out of the trip months before. She knew where the spare key was kept, which brick was loose behind the shed. She'd spent Thanksgiving with Mason's family—his parents, his brothers, their wives, his younger sister—but hadn't been back since. They'd been so nice. She hated it. She wasn't in love with Mason and it didn't seem fair, all that warmth. All that generosity made her sick to her stomach. All the ways she wasn't gracious.

The afternoon of the wedding, Vivian wandered in and out of rooms, taking photographs from the thresholds. When she'd used up the roll, she mostly sat at the dining room table and thought about that holiday. Sometimes she wished she could go back. Sometimes she missed how Mason's fingers stung her everywhere he touched, from the softest, untoned parts of her inner thighs to her wrists.

By evening, she gave up. She'd miscalculated how full of regret grief could make you, even if the grief had more to do with abstract longing than desire for a particular thing. She hadn't been in love with Mason, but she had wanted to be in love with him, and that meant she couldn't stay there like a stranger, which was the only way she allowed herself to stay anywhere. The only rule she had. She left the house as soon as it turned dark. Slid the brick in place and walked all the way to the bus station.

Back inside, Vivian flipped through the newspaper while she waited for the water to boil. Death notices, D-8; she skimmed columns for her name. Olivia M. Frommer, 36, survived by two daughters, a husband, a mother, grandmothers on both sides. Richard Nelson Fost, born 1927; survived by wife, Ava Fost, and stepson, Edward Case. Morgan Vargas Fitzgerald: 62, no survivors. This was Vivian's sad math, a fucked up game of points for the number of times her name and its variants appeared in the daily obits. First name proper was five. Names like Victoria, Vera, Vernon, Violet, Veronica were two. Foster was five points. Something like Fost counted once, and so did Olivia, because it contained Liv which resembled Viv. Middle name, half-point. Significant combinations or listings with her initials in order counted three points. VMF. One for each. That was how Vivian kept track of how close she was to dying. The fewer points the better. Each name that didn't match hers reduced her odds a little. That morning she counted three, and three was safer than ten.

Three was safer than ten. So Vivian left the house. Helen had mentioned a market nearby and pointed the way downtown, so she headed in that direction. She would establish a routine. Routine established purpose, a trick Vivian had learned to feel less like a visitor. Though, if she was being honest about it, community and stability weren't what she sought from her profession. This time felt different, if she couldn't exactly pinpoint how. But she noticed it as she walked—zipping her jacket against the damp, pulling the collar close at her neck—that she didn't feel the familiar drumming urgency to be anonymous, an outsider on the periphery slipping in and out of towns, giving fake names to fellow subway passengers, baristas, guys at bars. Here was a place, apparently, where someone could just vanish into thin air. What else could happen in a place like that.

At the market she weighed grapefruits. There was an announcement: reduced cakes. Vivian paced the aisles looking for the bread, found it, chose multiple grains. At the checkout she touched the slick corner of a celebrity magazine but did not buy it. She handed over her twenty-dollar bill and said thank you for the change.

On her walk back to the house, Vivian counted eight cicada shells. It was the season of nostalgia, August turning into September, almost her birthday, which was their birthday. She could almost forget she had a brother, since they hadn't been in touch for years. He was obscured, he was part time, he was in hiding. He was a mime. He was no forwarding address/no longer at this address/undeliverable. He was a postcard back in March that said *I am an exhibit at the state fair.* They were twins, but that didn't mean much that Vivian could vouch for. They weren't psychically connected. Vivian and Seth weren't aligned in some intrinsic, magical twin way and never had been. All they had in common was their gift for evasion. It was hereditary, in their family—the one quality you could point to that connected them. Evasive, evading, evaded. *He evaded the law. He evaded the question.* It was their mother's fault—she was the queen of evasion, having grown up ringside after seasonal ringside, the perma-costumed daughter of parents who worked the small-time carnivals. The names of those setups were fixed in her memory from stories her mother told: Bayside Marvels (New Madrid, MO); Land of Wonders (Carbon, UT); Point Mercenary Daylong Enchantments (Sulphur, LA). And here it was, the end of another summer. The two-headed calf was stumbling his final parade around the ring. The fire eater's awkward teenage assistant was dismantling the portable coaster, trying to forget the acne blushing painfully over half his face.

Vivian hardly heard the footsteps before someone rushed past her, running down the sidewalk. He would've run her over if she'd moved left; the person was oblivious. Startled into pausing there on the sidewalk, she watched as he dodged off. Lanky guy, dark sweatshirt; dark pants—she lost sight of him quickly.

She was almost at the house, Helen's house, when she spotted him again up ahead, a black sweatshirt turning down a driveway, jogging up to the side door of a green foursquare. He waited there on the porch a few seconds, then disappeared inside.

Dropping the match was easy.

The flame grew, peeling into the air as the match tip crumbled, and right as the last bit of it fell to flame—the orange creeping so close to his thumb the skin there began to glow—he dropped it. Opened the pinch of forefinger and thumb that held it steady and let go. The match caught the cardboard lip and flung into a hundred sparks, a thousand sparks, streaking through the boxes propped on the Dumpster until the whole thing was burning.

It was easy.

Ronny took off. The sound of his feet pounding the ground, pounding the dead leaves, was nothing compared to the blood knocking in his ears. He catalogued the items he passed as he ran, mostly to keep from turning around and looking. The woods edging the parking lot were full of things. Pabst Blue Ribbon cans, some forties, an empty bottle of Wild Irish Rose, a red baseball cap poking through the moldy leaves, an assortment of paper products—shredded napkins, grease-stained bags, flattened coffee cups. Ronny ran through the cold afternoon, gritting his teeth, breathing through his nose, eyes on the ground. Gray sleeve cut from a long-sleeved shirt. White plastic bag. White Styrofoam cup.

A cramp jerked his side, that familiar running stitch, and caused him to double over finally and brace against a tree. Head spinning, eyes hot, he was less than a mile from the fire still. He looked up—blackbird, shred of sky—had to keep going, get out of there.

His father stood over the stove in an ex-cowboy's brown plaid shirt, stirring something with one hand while the other held a section of newspaper up to his face. Ronny paused on the front porch before going in, catching his breath and watching through the kitchen window. His father looked small standing there like that, like he'd aged ten years in five months. He was going blind—the doctors expected him to lose eighty percent of his vision by the end of the year—and forgetting things. Like the tumor was a cloud that had settled its fog over half his brain instead of just a thumbtack behind his left eye, which is how they'd said it, a thumbtack. Ronny shut the door, dialed the deadbolt back into place.

"Ron," his father said from the stove, "there you are."

"Hey," Ronny said, and sat down at the kitchen table.

He had to calm down, cut it out, but who knew how far it would spread before someone stopped it—or no one stopped it—it was nearing winter, the trees were dying and the leaves were already dead, piles of dead leaves everywhere, everything could catch. He gripped the seat of his chair, the place where a long nail was wedged in at the wrong angle, and pressed his finger hard onto the point, held it there; the stab of pain calmed him a little, gave him something to focus on: the possibility of tetanus.

From the kitchen table he could see into the dining room, which they didn't use anymore. There were piles of things stacked across the table. Papers, books, clothes to be donated to Goodwill; junk mail, real mail, a bag of apples gone soft. They didn't gather there for meals now that it was just Ronny and his father. Not that they ever had. But the mathematical reality was that two people didn't gather. Three gather. Nine gather, twenty-five. But ever since Pete was gone, and his mother and Ronny moved out, that room was done for. Now Ronny was back, and they were down to two again, and two, basically, meet and divide. Nothing to keep them from the smallness of themselves. That was the thing Ronny didn't get—year after year the people around him continued to separate themselves out of the lives they were connected to. Like cells dividing, separating, multiplying. Like mitosis. That whole dining room could be a stain, an evolutionary cycle to be smeared on a slide and studied under better light. Fuck. Ronny had expected it to be emptied out by now, at least, but his father hadn't touched it. The meantime hadn't changed anything. It was depressing.

"Have you thought more about the job, Ron?" His father was talking to him from behind the refrigerator door, moving jars.

"Think it might be good for you, good opportunity, get you back in the swing of things."

Sure. Ronny had thought about it. But the job was a fucking joke. It was janitorial—some lab needed housekeeping. A job that had been open probably for months and lingered, unfilled. It was embarrassing, honestly, but he couldn't exactly go back to the Jungle, of course, no way. His boss had called a couple times when he didn't show up for two shifts in a row, but hadn't phoned since, which basically meant the coast was clear, but where did that leave him: not anywhere. Something had to give.

His eye caught Pete's sweatshirt draped over a dining room chair. Its light blue matched the blue strobes of the wallpaper flowers. He tried not to let certain facts register. He concentrated on the fact of the sweatshirt's blueness, the objective color of it rather than the powdery blue of skin that turns to pallor.

Obviously one of the stacks on the table was mail. Probably all Pete's mail was still arriving. It had been, what, a little over a year and a half, and he wouldn't put it past his father to just keep bringing it in. The magazine subscription, for example, month after month it would come. It takes a lot of energy to stop the momentum of an already-paid-for lifetime subscription of *Road Cycling* addressed to your dead son.

"Soup?" His father asked, placing the newspaper down on the counter. Clam chowder.

"Thanks," he said, distracted.

It was too late to go back. It was out of his control. It wasn't his.

Steam plumed from the bowl like breath through cold air and Ronny, who didn't eat meat, didn't even eat fish, found that he was starving.

Vivian Merritt Foster was working at the candle factory the night she disappeared, ladling paraffin wax into pillar molds on the late shift. At precisely eleven minutes past the hour, witnesses reported a visitor approaching the east entrance. Cameras recorded a figure exiting the facility twenty minutes later, unaccompanied, just a flash there and gone against the background of asphalt and chainlink. According to the manager on duty, Vivian had gone on break just before midnight, twenty-five minutes before the unknown visitor appeared on camera. When the night crew left, the sky was pitch black and Vivian was still gone. A cool, persistent breeze stirred the leaves on their branches, silkened the skin of the workers' short-sleeved arms as they spilled out across the parking lot. As they patted down pockets and handbags, looking for their keys.

Vivian ran water in the bathroom sink. The mirror above the sink was old, bent her reflection in some places and flattened it in others. She looked half normal and half far away regardless of where she stood. The breeze cleaved through the cracked window and rattled the glass against its frame, the rush of cold mixing with the dry radiator heat. Six names in the morning paper and three matched her initials exactly, VMF + VMF + VMF, which meant nine. She buttoned her sweater up to the neck, a flutter in the mirror that caught her attention. That working of button into buttonhole; the steadiness and precision of it. Her hands in the mirror looked like her mother's, the long fingers, wide knuckles, the pale wrist against shirt cuff. Whatever it is that contains illness, or makes illness unable to be contained anymore, and makes the tremors start—you could see it in the hands first, in the way they faltered or grasped, because hands give the body away. They become dumb, stutter, slow. What if it was hereditary? She was terrified that it might be hereditary. If she could solve the cause of it, maybe she could bilk the onset, because her mother hadn't always been crazy. After her carnival childhood, she'd left her parents, left the road, got emancipated, and went to high school. She graduated, moved to Berlin. Her visa expired; she returned to the states. She gave birth to Vivian and Seth when she was twenty-five, a single mother.

And Vivian remembered ordinary years. Regular stories, regular days at the park, regular Band-Aids, regular birthday cakes. Vague years of ordinary dinners, ordinary arguments, ordinary jobs. She was a secretary, a maid, a grocery store cake decorator; sometimes she kept two jobs at once, sometimes three.

Everything had been average and everything had been unremarkable, for all those days. Vivian and Seth had spent their childhood in a series of putty-colored apartments with interchangeable floor plans. The drab walls held gummy stains, indeterminate smudges like eraser scuff. They stayed in the apartment on Three Pines Terrace the longest. Three Pines Terrace with the thin walls and the single deadbolt latch, where the mail got delivered to a central community mailroom, which was the basement of the rental office. One time when she went to the mailroom, she was maybe twelve, Vivian had barged in on the maintenance officer having sex with the woman who always stood in front of the corner market, the one where you could play lotto and use food stamps to get beer. There was an old, slouch-cushioned armchair pushed up to the wall. Ratty carpet barely covered the concrete floor.

Three Pines Terrace was an arrangement of stucco buildings in block formation with a courtyard at the center and unwieldy shrubs growing ragged around the perimeter. Besides Three Pines there wasn't much for a couple miles, just slack marshes punctuated by a bait shop and a Cash 4 Cars lot.

About a mile before the car lot, there was an abandoned house. Cracks at the eaves left pools of rainwater after storms; windows, busted, ushered in cold wind; the staircase creaked loudly, the stairs dipped noticeably at trespassing weight. It was kind of grand, hulked up from the plot of overgrown ivy and snake-thick roots, and one day, when Vivian's mother said, "Pack your bags, we're going on vacation," that was where she meant. They were so young—maybe five or six—that the three-and-a-half miles from Three Pines must have felt suitably far from home, and the days they spent camping in the enormous, shadowy living room were perfectly removed from the rest of their lives. They took a tent and camping stove and canned food, and their mother was as close to joyful as they'd seen her, not scared of anything, not paranoid. She made soup and told them about Vesta, goddess of fire, and sea ghosts called Ashrays; flashlights on the tent made flames and waves.

Then they left. Crept back through the tangled yard, tripping over knots and roots, hoisting that crappy tent. After that vacation, they never returned. Vivian sensed that something had shifted, something that would prevent them from returning, would make returning impossible. They moved. The new apartment was smaller but roughly the same, with thin walls and plastic mini-blinds that always snapped loose from their cord.

Nothing was remarkable. Most things were the same. The years passed.

And then, one day, her mother put on a pair of thin white gloves cut to the elbows, took to her bed and did not leave her room for days, then weeks, lights off and the curtains pulled. Months passed. It was spring. There was no way to explain it: she'd stopped. Stopped cooking, stopped leaving, stopped working. She drew a check from the state and hunkered down. Called it witnessing. Called it preparing. She sat in the armchair and smoked, letting the ash build. She wouldn't take off the gloves, refused to touch things with bare hands. Wouldn't take the medication the doctors gave her, little sample boxes stuffed in her purse. Her hands shook. They were bad doctors, she said, they were men in coats who would kill her. The locks on the house got changed. *Evade, evasive, evasion.* Vivian didn't know what to do. The house got cold. It was winter. It was another spring.

One morning, riding the bus to junior high, a car accident had traffic tied up and detoured. Along the new route, Vivian saw the house and realized with dread it was where they'd camped. There in a brackish pocket of forest. It was dilapidated, slanted low, with an anemic front porch that swung away from the wood siding and smashed windows. She couldn't believe it.

And that house is where she went when, a few months later, she returned home from school to find her mother stockpiling nonperishables in the living room, building a whole color-coded wall of cans that already stacked halfway to the ceiling. It must have taken the entire day, which meant her mother had skipped work for the second time that week. She had a job at a factory clothing outlet back then, tagging polo shirts and pinning imperfect turtlenecks to mannequins. Vivian said why didn't you go to work, and her mother said what she'd said the last time. Who cares about shirts, it's too late. She stacked more cans. Vivian left, overwhelmed and claustrophobic. She wasn't thinking where she was going until it occurred to her that she was walking toward the junior high and that she would pass the abandoned house if she kept walking east, and she kept walking east.

That was the year things changed. Vivian learned how to cook. How to clean, how to leave. She kept the word *evasion* in the back of her throat, made it the name for a new disease.

The movie theatre was a fifteen-minute walk from the house and easy to find—seven blocks east, then maybe four blocks north—across from a 24-hour pharmacy that rarely stayed open past ten. The theatre was a boxy two-story that held firmly to its crumbling street corner. The ticket booth glowed.

Vivian considered her options. The showing she was about twenty minutes late for was a Hindi film. The poster for it, hanging next to Tickets and spotlighted by a flickering bulb, showed a woman wrapped in a red sari, from the elbows up, one of her eyes reflecting a fence of bars all linked up to form a tiny cage, like a thimble basket. Vivian bought a ticket and passed through the lobby—threadbare rose carpet, faded fleur de lis wallpaper and dim chandeliers—up a short spiral staircase to auditorium two, which was empty though the movie played anyway, sifting a boisterous soundtrack through the aisles and over all the vacant seats.

In the film there was a ceremony. One of the daughters of the first family, Chitra, was going to marry the son of the man who walked with a cane. Chitra, the woman from the poster. On the terrace when the rain started: a deluge that conjured a sudden river. A locket shoved hastily inside a drawer. Sheet of black hair braided patiently into an elaborate crown. Lotus blossoms spun downstream. The clouds gathered. A woman lit candles then placed them one by one in barrel-shaped lanterns. A can of condensed milk, folded into the bowl of flour. The clock struck four. She was kneeling. She was on her hands and knees sifting through the dirt, trying to unbury something. Or bury something.

Halfway through the film the theatre door opened. Vivian assumed it was an usher staking out his ten-minute break. Instead it was another moviegoer, a guy who walked down to the front and slid into a seat, which felt to Vivian mildly disturbing, an interruption that displaced her privacy even in the dark room. On the screen, another suitor had arrived. When he opened a suitcase a cloud of finches shimmied out, then took off, soaring over the crowd of guests. And now the new family, the man with the cane, his wife in perfectly draped silk, her bangles slipping as she reached to tap his shoulder—Vivian found that she could watch the action and simultaneously keep the guy up front in her peripheral view. He restlessly leaned forward, leaned back.

A finch in someone's pocket; a boy with a comb in his mouth. A third sister, possibly a cousin, threaded a needle and strung a palmful of teeth on a ribbon one by one. The final scene was in grayscale, someone tossing a fistful of birdseed at someone else's feet.

She watched the credits trail over the screen, cursive that scrolled to fog letters, and pretended to be deep in concentration about something when she saw the guy standing, walking up the aisle, headed her way. Turning to reach for her coat just as he got to her row and moved past, she listened to the door swinging closed behind him, a dull thud. Her face burned with the recognition that she knew the guy, after all, because he was her neighbor.

Vivian stood squinting in the dusty lobby, her eyes slow to adjust to the new brightness. The running guy and Vivian were the only two people around, besides the teenager who left the box office with a push broom and a woman at concessions. When Vivian came out of the theatre, Ronny had been talking on the payphone stationed across the lobby, between the restrooms. Vivian bent to tie her shoes which turned out to be boots and did not have laces. She adjusted the knees of her tights instead, pulling straight the ribbing. She was buying time. When he hung up, Vivian hesitated, then surprised herself by waving. He shrugged and headed across the room to where she stood, the ice maker grinding to a halt behind them.

"Hey, sorry to bother you, I was thinking you live on my street. Well I'm house-sitting, actually, so, where your neighbors live. I'm Vivian."

"Vivian," he hesitated, "Hey. I'm Ronny."

"Yeah," Vivian said, for no reason.

Ronny nodded, thought about something. "You're staying in the house across the street then. I heard about that, the professor."

"I moved in a few days ago," she nodded.

Ronny had never met the professor. Paul and Helen had only lived on that street for about a year, a little more than the time Ronny had been gone. He remembered the moving trucks back then, and he remembered the cop cars that came a few weeks ago, started showing up in the mornings, one undercover and one squad.

His manner was quiet and a little distracted or preoccupied with something else, more than that lobby and whatever she would manage to say next. He was only vaguely interested, not committed to the details, she could tell. Ronny wore a brown sweater, had longish hair that was growing shaggy. There was something familiar and withdrawn about his face, and careless, the beginning of a beard. A patch sewn in wrong over his pants knee. He was slim, but rugged, like a boat maker. Like a boat maker who rose early, heaved planks for hours at the lip of the river and didn't own a TV.

"Well," he said, a suggestion they should move on. An usher was locking the bank of doors behind them; a manager carried a clipboard back to the registers. It was late.

Outside he paused to light a cigarette. He wasn't supposed to have a lighter. But you could get your hands on anything. You got by. He needed to go back and check the place out but with Vivian following him . . . He took a long drag and started walking home. She fell in slightly behind.

"How'd you know where I was staying?" Vivian said to the back of his sweater.

He shrugged. She watched the orange spark between his fingers lift back and forth.

"Saw you the other day," he said, "Taking the newspaper in."

She nodded. So he'd noticed her. It was an idea she felt in her stomach: she wasn't the only one paying attention, or hadn't been. He was obviously in a hurry to do something, though, and she was losing him to it.

"So where's the fire," she said.

He turned, quickly, checked her face for something, some sign, who knows, and went on walking.

"What do you mean," he said, not like a question.

She'd said the wrong thing, of course; she'd never gotten the hang of small talk, of how to be casual enough with all the questions you were supposed to use to learn about another person. There was an etiquette to it, a pattern that seemed to be natural for everyone else but which Viv ruined, overthinking every word. Overanalyzing every exchange, aware there were shortcuts and codes, but what were the rules, it was a gamble. So she was always saying dumb things. Really, what it came down to was the peculiar deficiency of not understanding how to be known by anyone. She didn't want to give too much away. In fact, she was embarrassed to even be seen bending down to the tray of a vending machine, retrieving a bag of Fritos from the drop bin. How could a person stand to always be seen desiring, and taking. Not just food, either—anything coveted. To Viv, every kind of hunger felt vulgar, and that was an embarrassing kind of shame.

To Ronny she said, "What's the rush, when I saw you before you were running, that's all, now you're walking so fast, it was a dumb joke you know—forget it."

She'd caught him off guard and it was uncomfortable, a shift that put him under inspection, because when had she seen him before tonight, he wondered, running?

"Yeah, well," he finally shrugged. Something bothered him. Half-heartedly he tried but could think of nothing to say.

Ronny kept his head down. They walked in awkward silence, got past another block without talking. Ronny smoked as he walked, and pictured each house they passed going up in flames, thinking how you could see every second ending if it was set on fire. Every second burned off the present.

The Doctor was looking for the blueprint. Drawer after drawer he lumbered his way around the office, a map of the ribcage in his head. Last night he'd dreamed the wings again and the dream gave him an idea. More of the rib, dismantled, would make the wing frame more flexible; keep the frame too stiff and motor impulse would suffer. Of course! Stiffness was fine for soaring, was preferable even, but would be detrimental for ascent.

On his second lap around the room, after considerable rifling through the file cabinet, he found it. He unrolled the blueprint and smoothed it flat across the table. With his charcoal pencil he scratched a panel from the ribcage and shaded it in. In this manner he sharpened the planned angle and extended the webbing, which would be stretched from the fat around the torso and rewoven. He sketched the incision and diagrammed the positioning of the scalpel and the wing, penciled in notations about which measurements to take later. Brilliant, yes, it was, it was making sense. The Doctor studied the drawing with its additions for a minute more, then shuffled back across the room to the desk and filed it safely away in the only drawer he could lock with a miniscule key.

It was late afternoon and he was off to his rounds. First patient was Kneecap. He'd skewered his leg on an access road at 120 miles per hour when he lost control of his motorcycle. Re-networking the threads of ligament beneath the new cap had been laborious work; so far the graft seemed to be tightening as well as could be anticipated. The rest was up to nature. Nature would take its course. For starters, traces of tar and mica remained in the shin and the thigh. For the Doctor, this conjured visions of metallic skin. Impervious to scarring, he thought. Chain mail.

Next patient was Nose, the retired debutante from Orlando. She'd come in for a reformative nose job and he'd reshaped it, hopefully for the last time. It was set perfectly but due to complications he would keep her overnight. Besides, it would be good to keep her around if only since, incidentally, she was his focal point in the argument he planned to wage for the Board that afternoon, the abbreviated version of which went:

If repeat elective cosmetic surgery is legitimized medically and ethically and according to strict guidelines (he had memorized his part of the dialogue), *those same guidelines must conceive of—must fathom* (fathom, yes) *the various and important possibilities of elective surgery to challenge the extremes of the human condition beyond vanity: a re-envisioning of the human condition.*

It was elementary; actually, it was practical. Of course there were no counterarguments for fixing gruesome aberrations—Kirschner wires and cutaneous reconstruction—or for amending physical hardships with, for example, cleft palate surgery; of course not: the body begs swift repair. Waging normality, though, and spending thirty-something years reinforcing the status quo when there was more to do—when they were long past the time, long overdue, for invention—that was a shame he could no longer endure. In fact, it was downright ludicrous to continue to endure—good God, it was a burden. To be sure, a body that isn't broken doesn't require fixing. But invention, enhancement; the unprecedented adaptations the human form might withstand, to think of it: the new body, the super-human body—*that* was the work of the extraordinary. That was what the Doctor's tools were for. He (for one) was not there to trade in vanity, he would make that clear. No, his oath was to restore the delicate system of body with function. *But.* Reinventing that system—yes. Yes, they must.

Shuffling down the corridor he had gruff nods for the orderlies and nurses and residents he passed. What he looked like to them, he knew, was an old man, unstylish and disheveled with or without his surgeon's coat and clipboard. They had no idea what he was planning, what miracle he was setting into motion just a few doors down the hall from their respective offices and labs. They did not, could not, fully grasp his—his *monumental*—expertise as a plastic surgeon. He could tell they were blind to his immensity; he knew they thought he was nuts, and old—as old as their grandfathers, in some cases. And yet, his delicate stitch work and his impeccable bone sculpting were renowned in reconstructive units worldwide. He was cited in their texts, for Christ's sake. His reputation was considerable. They were defenseless when confronted with his genius. They were held captive by his genius. And, most unfortunately for them, the Doctor thought, most unfortunately for them, they could never, the lot of them, fully comprehend nor prepare for what would come next. Because what came next . . . what came next would be his glory.

Overnight it had gotten colder, shifting the last week of November into an official cold snap that began in the earliest hours as ropes of sleet and by mid-morning glazed the roads over completely, shut everything down. By early afternoon, branches and power lines overlapped in a shiny grid. The storm went on and on. Viv had spent the entire day in bed. Her encounter with Ronny the night before had left her feeling depressed and out of sorts. When she finally left the bedroom to put the kettle on, she hadn't even bothered dressing, just buttoned a long-sleeved shirt over what she'd slept in, a thin-as-paper slip and her underwear. She was, she decided, done with the world of other people. She settled in the living room with her tea, covered herself in the guestroom quilts, and flipped through an issue of *National Geographic* from 1971, the only thing she could reach without moving from the couch. She read an article about Lenin called "The Social Catastrophe," and didn't think about Ronny. She didn't think about Ronny. She didn't know Ronny. She had no reason to feel as if she'd lost something. She was fine. She was fine in the house of a missing man, fine in a town that wasn't hers, fine on her own. She didn't exactly need other people in her life, and didn't exactly miss them when they were gone, except for certain fleeting, companionable parts of them. She didn't miss the entire, overlapping history of a person because people were generally messy and selfishly dramatic and took up too much room. Vivian preferred not to commit to drawn-out, exhausting relationships and endless compromises and dim stains on bed sheets. It had always seemed like something her exes appreciated about her, how she didn't altogether want them in ways they didn't know how to be needed yet. They were happy to test the give and take, the physical measures of desire, and that was all, and that was enough for her, too. Nights, Vivian found, were easy. Mornings were unavoidable—naked bodies done with their nakedness and cold, and unfamiliar socks balled up on the floor, and someone politely pretending to sleep while someone else politely turned toward the door—but those were short-lived. A person would eventually be dressed and you could lock the door behind them. Maybe that was partly what this was about—it had been months since she'd slept with anyone—but no, not that, it was something else, more obscure than sex. She'd spent twenty-five minutes with Ronny, tops, making a fool of herself. What kept him on her mind? What kept him.

Vivian had fallen asleep, and when she woke the room was pitch black and colder. She was disoriented and it took her a minute to understand the power had gone out. The streetlights were dark, the houses across the street were dark; lights out down the block. She could see inside the room enough to make her way across it, but from the hallway, she had to feel her way to the kitchen.

Silverware, Tupperware, plastic cups—she opened every drawer looking for a flashlight. She skipped the pantry, which was enormous and impossible to sort through in the dark. She was kneeling, searching inside a cupboard when she heard a knock at the door. She waited, maybe it was nothing, maybe it would go away—but there it was again, louder. Shit. She groped her way down the hall to the stairs and then down the stairs and the knocking got more insistent. She tripped down the last step and stumbled to the front door. She lifted a corner of the panel that covered the window, saw Ronny standing there, and remembered she was hardly dressed. Of course, she thought. Of course.

She pulled the door open partway, propping it with her elbow.

"Hey, sorry, Vivian—Viv—everything okay over here?"

He looked down at her, squinted to see past the doorway.

"The storm's getting worse. No one's got power; I know it's a weird time to stop by, but I knew you were alone here. Well I figured at least, and thought I'd check, you know," he said.

The sleet had mostly stopped but the wind was harsh, howling across the power lines like a miserable animal.

"Yeah, I'm fine, just looking for candles, a flashlight, I don't . . ."

Her voice trailed off as she willed herself not to shiver.

"Want some help?" He pulled the cords tighter on his jacket hood. It was too cold to make him stand there. She stepped back from the door to make room and they stood in the cold foyer.

"I've been looking in the kitchen," Vivian said, realizing she could see her breath, "But no luck."

She folded her arms across her chest, self-conscious and freezing.

"It's upstairs," she said, and followed him up.

In the kitchen Ronny kept his jacket on. At first they didn't talk and the only sound in the room was cupboards closing and drawers rolled back on dull casters. Outside the tree branches cracked in the wind, and the sharpness of the ice snapping as branches split in half was an exaggerated sound. It didn't make sense that Ronny was in the kitchen, whammo, just like that. Why had he bothered, after she'd pissed him off. What did he want, she thought. But she was glad for the company.

"Hey, I think I found it," Ronny said, as he brought something out from the drawer under the stove.

A flashlight. He shook it to see if it had batteries and switched it on. A weak light pulled across the kitchen floor. "Well, this might be it," he said. "All you've got."

"Well," she said, "thanks." She was sitting on the kitchen floor; she'd been looking in all the bottom drawers. Ronny stood the flashlight in the middle of the room so it threw a spotlight on the ceiling and barely lit up the part of the kitchen where Vivian sat.

"It's going to get so cold in here," she said. It was already cold.

"Yeah," Ronny said.

"Yeah," she said again, agreeing with herself, with him, not really knowing what to do. She could imagine how you waited it out: touch and go.

He sat down across from her, leaned against the island.

"Last night," she started but Ronny interrupted.

"I'm sorry, is it weird I'm here?"

"It's—fine," she said. "It's surprising. But it's nice, to have a visitor, I haven't met anyone here."

"I didn't want you to think—I just had to go, last night. I was just—late for this thing—"

"No, it was stupid," Viv said.

"It was nothing, anyway," he said. "Should I go? If you're fine and I'm . . . interrupting."

Nothing about Ronny was too precise—his hair was wild enough to require that he sometimes shake it out of his face, and in another day or so he'd have a beard—so he seemed soft, despite looking rugged, and weary, as if he'd been hiking for weeks. He waited for Vivian to ask him to stay. He didn't want to give the wrong impression, but it was a test to remain completely oblivious of her there; especially since it seemed—it was hard to see—that she was dressed in basically a long flimsy shirt—like she was getting ready to take a shower or go to bed. He didn't want to stare. But he could confirm, as he'd suspected last night, that she was lovely in a way. She was somewhat Victorian seeming—he could imagine her wearing button-down blouses and wool skirts in the swelter of August—but she was also disheveled and oblivious to her valentine mouth and her large eyes, which were dark stare factories. Her hair was pulled back, messy, in a ponytail.

"I wouldn't mind company," she said, "and—have you eaten? I haven't had dinner."

She opened the refrigerator. A block of cheese, several imported beers. All the rest was leftovers from Helen, ugly-sad rubber containers of what looked like party food from a wake. Casserole fractions. Pulled meat.

"Help yourself," Vivian said. "There's food like someone died."

She brought out the cheese on a plate and found some crackers. Opened a bottle of beer. Ronny fumbled at the counter with a bottle of whiskey, pouring into a mug. A symphony mug, because Helen and Paul probably donated.

"I have quilts in my room," Viv said, and they took the flashlight down the hall to the guest room. At the window, she pressed her forehead to the glass and cupped her hands to look outside. The street, the trees, the telephone wires and power lines: everything was lacquered in ice. The wind had slowed, was pushing the trees around less violently from the sound of things.

Vivian moved across the room, set her beer down on the floor next to the bed.

"It's warmer here," she said, getting in and gathering up the blankets, "Come on."

She made room for him, patting the mattress beside her. He sat down so that his back was against the wall and his legs stretched out over the edge in front of him.

"So," Ronny said, holding up his symphony mug like cheersing. She couldn't see from there but bars of music were stamped around the lip.

"Tell me something," Vivian suggested.

Ronny didn't know what to say.

"Anything, tell me something about this place."

She tugged at the hem of his sweatshirt, the scrap she could reach without moving.

He drank again, it was warm, and thought about what he could tell her. What good thing he could tell her. The quarry came to mind. It was remarkable, a deep gorge in the earth, so huge it was unbelievable unless you saw it for yourself, and even then you felt so dwarfed it was hard to look down when you were standing at the edge of it. But it was manmade. And thinking about the quarry meant thinking about the fire, and there you had it: this town, he wanted to burn it. Last night when he'd left her and started back out, he'd gone to assess the damage, and when he'd gotten there he'd regretted it because his boss was there too, the office all lit up blazing like afternoon, and he knew he might've seriously fucked up. Was his boss sleeping there now? Pulling surveillance? It could've been seriously fucking bad. He'd stayed back in the woods, back of the shop, and from there all he could tell was the shop seemed normal, still standing. That's what he wanted: to fuck shit up, but fuck it up within reason, not obliterate it.

"Well," he said, "this town—"

"There's got to be something," Viv said.

"I'm telling you, this town—is, where I grew up. Right across the street. I did everything here, all of school, all the stupid milestones, right, first drugs, first dates, first petty crimes. And then I left, now I'm back, and all I can think is this town gets fucking smaller."

"And," Vivian said.

"That's it."

"No ghost stories or tales of misery and fortune that get passed around? Nothing that used to scare the shit out of you when you were a kid," she said.

"Besides this?" he joked, indicated the room and meant the whole house.

A man was missing. A power outage, two strangers in a house. The dumb story where the caller is calling from inside the house and cut the fuse box on purpose. Vivian didn't want to think about it.

"Why'd you come back?" she said.

Ronny hesitated, aware that he should lie. He should definitely deny the past two years, every lame mistake. Everything they could arrest him for. He could have said anything, put it all behind him, could've just changed the subject, and he would never know why he didn't, why he told Vivian everything right from the start—later, looking back, the effect she had on him would still be confusing—but he told her all of it. Why he left, the fires, Pete's accident, his parents' divorce, moving out with his mother, moving back to town. He'd never told anyone this stuff. How for a month they made him see a counselor at the center but the counselor was a grad student, an intern, and Ronny was a shortcut, an easy write-off. When Ronny refused to talk, the counselor played solitaire while Ronny sat staring out the window until his hour was up, week after week. The first fire, Ronny told her, was before Pete's accident. Or actually, it might have been—which Ronny hated to realize, it made him guilty—the fire might have begun, might have still been burning, at the exact moment the truck approached, skidding, Pete's wheel clipped and twisted and going under, flipping him off, flipping the bike over the edge of the road—

He couldn't think about it. And he hadn't planned it out; he'd just done it. Lit the match, stuck it in the trashcan outside the high school's shop room, touched the tiny flame, just the tip, to a wad of paper under sawdust, a scrunched up bag that probably held some kid's lunch a few hours earlier. Ronny pictured the perfect sandwich square as he dropped the match, slowly turned, took three slow steps before sprinting into the woods. Where Ronny hid, just inside the stand of trees, he could see clear across campus to the track and field. No runners on the track yet; Coach Driver would still be going over meet times with them in the locker room. As Ronny watched, a janitor opened the back door and dumped a box into the trashcan. He remembered what happened, saw it playing out in slow motion: the thin flash of orange; the janitor stumbling back, shouting as he darted into the building; back again seconds later with a fire extinguisher, sinking the trash can in white foam. He watched, Ronny watched, and his knees got weak, he was sweating. The afternoon had been unseasonably warm, the sky a broad ribbon between clouds. The whole way home he'd felt it, the heat grazing his thumb as he took too long dropping the match. When he'd gotten home that afternoon there'd been a message from his father, calling from Bellsden. *There's been an accident Ron. It's Pete. It's Pete*, his voice breaking over the chirping loudspeaker that went emergency-emergency-emergency. All he remembered from the rest of that day was the hospital's generic hallways lined with pastel tiles: peach and yellow and pale blue. The fluorescent buzz overhead made him think of wasps. So cold inside the waiting room, so bright and deceptively clean when just being there made disease stir inside you, in your kneecaps, ankles, ears. It seeped in. Ronny had kept his hands in his pockets, stared straight ahead. Counted each door he passed. Nine until he got to Pete's room. Nine doors and he was the last brother left. Nine doors and he was at the end. Nine doors and his mother inside sobbing.

"He didn't wake up," Ronny told Vivian, "From the coma. It was pretty bad, the wreck was pretty bad." He went on about the days after—his parents' split, his mother's move to a larger city three hours away, his father's method of coping, which was a self-imposed amnesia, walking around acting like nothing had even happened. Each time he looked over at Vivian she was watching him expectantly, so he went on. He moved out to stay with his mother; it was a disaster; he quit going to class. He dropped out of high school the first semester of his senior year, washed dishes at a place called Spirits, spent all his money on shitty beer; his mother went on dates with men who wore spray tans and sports jackets with pocket squares. He got caught setting fires three separate times. The fourth was a close call—behind a convenience store, which would've meant endangerment, worse than arson, and he would have been held and charged—so he got a few months in juvie and community service, wearing an orange vest and picking up litter from the medians. He went back to his father's, even though he could've just taken off, gone anywhere. Couldn't explain why he was back. For now, he added, and knew it sounded like so much bullshit. He looked at Vivian, wishing he had more whiskey in front of him, cursing himself for having left the bottle in the kitchen.

"This was all a year ago, a little over a year ago, Pete's accident. His bedroom is exactly the same," Ronny said. "It feels like this kind of permanent funeral over there."

He picked up the mug again but it was empty. Put it down. He hadn't meant to make himself sound this pathetic.

"So fucking depressing," he said.

They were quiet for a while. Then Vivian reached for the flashlight and turned it off. The room went dark, except for the icy light floating in from the window, and she sat up, leaned over, and kissed him, kissed his cheek, and her lips were so soft, and her chin brushed against his earlobe as she pulled away and her hair smelled like cold leaves.

"I'm sorry," she said. Left the light off.

Ronny said, "No, you know—" He shrugged, "It's—"

He wanted her to come back, as if he could already feel that she was farther away or disappearing. She had that way about her, where she could move steady in one direction but instantly retreat.

He lowered himself next to her on the bed, facing her, his head on his propped up arm. It was getting colder. He gathered the quilt over them and they lay together, waiting for something to happen or not happen.

"I'm sorry," she said again.

"What for," he said. "There's nothing for you to be sorry for."

"Everything," Vivian said. "I'm sorry for all of it."

She meant it. She wanted to make it stop, to turn the switch that would bring on the next life. But the house stayed dark. Outside the storm carried on. She brushed her hand across his forehead, barely touching him, and he closed his eyes.

The ice storm lasted two days, and Ronny spent both with Viv, camped in the guest room. Ronny had returned to his father's house once to rally groceries, and his father—Ronny guessed he was in the library upstairs, buried in the paper—did not stir. Undisturbed. Was that Ronny's specialty, probably, being perpetually overlooked? Barely registering but in his wake: ashes, mud prints, discarded glove. Evidence of criminal intent. He was the kind of joker that summoned pity. What had Vivian said when he'd finished telling her? *I'm sorry.* He was at her mercy, which made him feel dumb and sort of miserable.

He lit a cigarette and tossed the lighter into the trash can. More evidence, he thought, as it clanked against the trash can's metal lip. He leaned against the wall and smoked, waiting out the five minutes before he had to report for work. The new arrangement. Another sign he was a loser: his father had pulled strings to get him hired, calling it a step in the right direction, pleased Ronny would not be returning to Concrete Jungle. "You see how this goes, Son"—he'd said at breakfast, at the table that was sticky with juice that dried where it spilled—"and who knows, maybe you'll study medicine yourself." His father had talked to a friend, an old fraternity brother who worked as a physical therapist at the hospital. He'd told him everything, his father said—"cleaned the slate"—because Ronny wouldn't have cleared security on his own.

All for a chance to sweep shit up. He took one more drag, picked a shred of tobacco from his bottom lip, and went inside.

He walked the busy halls looking for the elevator. People hustled in all directions, getting closer to getting things done. He rode up to the fifth floor with a group of silent nurses, wanting another cigarette immediately. He hadn't been back to the hospital since the last time he'd gone to see Pete in the ICU. Problem was, the whole hospital looked and smelled the same—it had that pale green, clinical smell of fear and business. Whatever else was there, that hospital green was there beneath it, in the sheets on the bed and the tiles on the wall. The pale green of last hope, lukewarm meals in the cafeteria, and visiting hours ending.

He was going to have to knock this the fuck off.

The custodial office had told him where to go. Down the hall, fifth floor, east wing. Ronny knocked on the door while turning the doorknob and stepping into the room. An older man in a lab coat sat with his back to the door, hunched over something, studying something with a magnifying glass.

"I'll be right with you," the Doctor muttered in a graveled voice, marking something down, shaking his head about it, and marking again.

"Now—" the Doctor turned to Ronny at the door while shoveling his glasses back on his face, "You're—Ron, is it?"

He shook Ronny's hand firmly. No nonsense. The Doctor sized him up, and Ronny wondered what he knew, what preceded him. It couldn't be good, because Ronny had a reputation. At best, he was considered a loner. *Difficult* was how they put it, meaning *Not terribly ambitious*. But he'd found out that what had happened to Pete gave him a free pass. He screwed up, and the neighborhood wives discussed it over coffee in well-appointed parlors, sharing news of his family's latest grief, and came to the same conclusion: *But his brother died, and then his mother left and his father is not quite right and what a terrible shame.* They'd always agree, pleased their own sons and daughters were practicing law and lobbying for rain forest protection and joining the Peace Corps in Uganda or Siberia or Kazakhstan, thankful Ronny was not their son.

"They've told me you will be, custodially speaking, in charge of my lab. And we need to keep this lab running, tight as a ship," the Doctor said. He shuffled to the back of the room, waving that Ronny should follow.

"So, Ron, this—" he handed over a key on a metal loop which he pulled from his pocket, and gestured to the shelves of cleaning supplies "—this is the broom closet."

And that was how Ronny became a janitor. He was issued a navy blue work shirt, a basic limited access entry/exit security badge, and a series of keys to unlock the doors of fifth floor east. Custodianship was pretty close to what he'd expected. He'd banked on the long, scuff-marked halls and the duct-taped mop handle, the routine of back and forth meandering while others rushed past, heads bent, coats flapping their knees. He'd banked on the antiseptic liquid dispensed from an industrial-sized container into an industrial-sized bucket, filled and dumped twice to cover the length of the corridor. He carried a set of master keys hooked to the loop of his work pants. Twenty-seven keys for twenty-seven office/closet/cabinet/washroom doors, plus the door to the south end fire escape. They jangled when he mopped, pushed the broom, sat down, stood up. Every small clanging reminding him of the series of tasks to which he'd committed. He got two smoke breaks and a lunch break, during which he stayed out of the hospital cafeteria and opted instead for the nearby diner where he could eat for two dollars and the ashtrays were shaped, for no particular reason, like flounder.

It was as ordinary a job as Ronny had ever had. He shuffled down the bleak hallway, counting squares of tile, dustpan in tow; shuffled back. It was routine. It was solitary. Not many patients on the floor. Every few days a stretcher would get wheeled through, empty, a nurse headed to the X-ray lab one floor down. A few times a visitor had gotten lost on the way to a patient's room, and Ronny had to redirect them to the elevators, but there wasn't much need, otherwise, for anyone to talk to him, or for him to ever speak.

Generic hour after generic hour, he wore the day out in increments of light physical labor, and though it was boring, at least he was moving around and not sitting there staring at blocks of cement anymore. And what more was it meant to be, really, besides what it was: a day job, a way to spend the hours he'd have to get through anyhow. Because if he wasn't at the hospital he'd have to be somewhere else. No way was he going to stay at home with his dad there, milling around in his old suits, lining up plastic army men on the mantle, shooting finger guns at them from across the room. Forget it. For now he might as well tab the scale and properly dispose of broken iodine vials.

When he went down for his break, he went out the parking deck side and crossed the lot to the benches that bordered a kind of fake, hospital-land park. He smoked and thought about her. The antique situation of her herringbone knee socks, the sweatshirt with the neck cut out that slipped, showing off part of her shoulder when she moved. Not something Ronny would ever notice but everything about Vivian was distinctive in a quiet, offhand way. Probably lots of the time she could be a wallflower, plain as any anonymous person standing shyly in a crowded room, with her monochromatic, slightly ill-fitting clothes; her peach Chapsticked lips. She looked like she lived in a different universe than the girls he knew and had grown used to in all their decorations: decaled palm tree and checkerboard nails and dangling earrings stacked at varying lengths up and down their perfect ears. Definitely sexy, he wouldn't deny it, but Vivian's unadorned loveliness was stranger. Out of place. He found himself getting distracted by thoughts of her throughout the day, as he polished the floor, inventoried the Doctor's scales, and took the stairs two at a time down to the basement. At least it kept him from tallying up all the things he might want to set on fire.

Vivian Merritt Foster drowned in Good Hope Lake. During the heat wave, late afternoon, solo captaining the boat down to the basin where the old prison barracks were, now mostly rotted to shacks. Around here, people joyride boats, leave the cars alone. Mostly ends okay but the storm broke out, no warning, and this boat wasn't a boat with a proper cabin but a skiff you shove right out of on rough waters, which came, rolling waves that pounded the docks—too far off—and the vessel. The rain pounded the splintering boat and the dreggy lake and went on and on and the lightning diagrammed the smokestacks through the dark, slashed the treetops. Vivian couldn't swim. She is survived by one known brother, Seth Everett Foster, most recently of California. She appears to have struggled to pen a letter to dry land in her last minutes, though no evidence thereof remains.

Most days Ronny didn't see the Doctor much. Early morning he'd be slouched over a set of papers or files or books at his desk until he was called away to surgery or to consult with a patient. Afternoons—late afternoon, when Ronny's shift was ending—he'd return to the lab to carry out some part of an experiment or do paperwork. Ronny usually took off when the Doctor came back to the lab since he seemed perpetually on the brink of irritation. And though the Doctor hardly offered a word in passing to Ronny, he muttered incessantly to himself as he worked, which gave Ronny the impression of being excluded from conversation, which made him feel paranoid. Made him duck out of the office to see about the broken soap dispenser in the unisex bathroom, or take a walk down to the supply room in the basement. And that was his new routine. Day after day Ronny showed up. Shift after shift Ronny completed his custodial tasks. He tried not to think, This is what I've become. This is who I am. He had to remind himself there was still time to turn it all around; there was still time before the relentless monotony killed him.

The size of things baffled Vivian. How much space a particular thing required of your life once you claimed it, for instance. The situation with her mother, and her mother's illness, was a gaping dirge. It was a road that dead-ended at a rope bridge, if the ropes were shorn and the bridge extended from an outcropping in Mongolia where cop cars weren't bound to pass for years and years. Seth on the other hand—somehow, even after all this time, he didn't take up much room, considering he was her only sibling and her twin. But his missing was more like a texture that overlaid the days as the days accumulated, not the hours. The hours were an entirely different situation. The hours belonged to Helen and Paul and the mystery that accounted for Paul's disappearance. Because even in Helen and Paul's absence, the house they left behind held the minor habits of their mornings and afternoons and evenings. The food in the pantry, the clothes in the hamper. The books and newspapers stacked in piles around the house. Helen and Paul were everywhere she looked. Every arrangement conveyed their persistent absence, which felt sinister. Vivian realized she was having a harder time settling in than usual, realized the house she was living in felt like a crime scene. She thought there must be clues in Paul's desk drawers, items that required fingerprinting. She should touch everything less. She should wear gloves.

If she wanted to, she could chalk it up to plain old anxiety, how she waited for Ronny to arrive every night, met him at the door, kept letting him in and letting him stay. The way her stomach felt. The way her face flushed every time she opened the door and saw him there. Maybe it wasn't excitement, it was relief. Except it was also excitement, and it was the kind of excitement she'd given up on feeling, the kind that overruled everything else, and the discovery that she wanted Ronny to take up space: that was the relief. The size of that relief: large enough to overlap the other sizable objects that had taken up residence inside her body, too. Even that dictionary of loss got eclipsed. The relief: so great it might buckle her ribs.

The Doctor swallowed the last lukewarm dregs of hospital coffee and tossed the cup in the trash. An extremely long night loomed before him. No point in going home just for the few—two, perhaps two and a half—hours he would toss and turn before he'd be driving back, heading in for morning rounds, afternoon research, and the evening he would spend on call. Better to stay. He'd get some rest in his office. He'd done it before. Lately he'd been doing it a lot, as a matter of fact. Ever since Lorraine left him. He worked too much, she'd said, had told him so over dinner at that ridiculous bistro she'd insisted on trying, the new ritzy place down on River. Well, so he was—too busy for marriage, too busy to keep Lorraine entertained, and apparently too busy, in fact, to even manage an excursion home at the end of every day. His project required his greatest attention, required every ounce and factor of his energy, and he held the tremendous burden of a brilliant design on his shoulders. His staggering vision. A once-in-a-lifetime vision—could no one tell? Regardless, staggering visions allowed no margin for error or interest, no time for anyone or anything else.

He reviewed his sketches and notes, arranged the graph paper across his desk in one long span. The wing tip that extended from the shoulder should be less rounded; he still needed more of an angle there. And the degree of the slope from shoulder to elbow—that would have to be taken into consideration when he developed the collapsibility mechanism. That was a challenge, determining how the device would retract the span of bones and skin quickly, as if by a tug of the muscle—although—he had the flash of an idea—could it not be as simple a mechanical effort as whatever that device was that commanded the retractable umbrella to fold and collapse? Using spokes instead of bones, and managing the spring lever tension . . . well, undeniably it was vulgar, but tweaked it could provide a dignified model, come to think of it. The Doctor made a notation. He hoped the boy, Ron, would prove a worthy assistant. It was hard to tell. He could use Paul's input, but who knew when he'd hear from

Paul again. The boy would have to work out, would have to be assistant enough in the meantime. He'd have to follow the Doctor's lead, and the Doctor knew his lead to be infallible—so what was the problem, after all? The Doctor reached for his coffee, then remembered it was gone, cup tossed in the trash, and corrected his gesture to adjust his glasses where they met his nose. He pulled a yellow legal pad from his desk—time to get started on the lecture—and wrote down *primitive appendage*. He wrote *landlocked*. He penciled in a webbed hand.

Ronny was avoiding his father. He'd been spending the nights at Vivian's—Helen and Paul's—and so far hadn't been asked by his father where he went every night. Of course, his father probably hadn't noticed he kept leaving. But living at home again made him feel scrutinized, like he was back in high school, and he was too fucking old to be there anymore—he knew guys his age who were married. That was the small town factor, mostly, but when you thought of it that way, that he could be married by now, Ronny knew it was time to get out. So not only was he avoiding his father to duck questions about his personal life (though, who was he kidding, what would his father have asked?)—he was avoiding his father because he didn't want to know if his father *hadn't* noticed how rarely he was home anymore. (Didn't he *get* how everything had changed? If that was the case, if he was that clueless, Ronny didn't want to know.) He wondered sometimes if maybe his father was actually waiting for Pete to come home, wander right back in through the front door, all his gear on. Because ever since Ronny had moved back in, his father stumbled through the days with a sort of steadfast refusal to appear less than perfectly content, his mouth pulled into a permanent half-smile. But his eyes seemed vacant. The other night, when Ronny was in his room gathering stuff for Vivian's, he'd heard someone knocking and looked up. It hadn't come from the door. He'd looked over, and there was his father, his face framed in his bedroom window and backlit by the streetlamp at the edge of the drive. Ronny opened the window to hear what he was saying.

"Dad," he'd said, "What the—"

"Thought I'd clean the windows up before hitting the sack," he'd said, matter-of-factly, holding up a dishtowel. He was hovering outside the window, twelve feet above ground, trying to clean the windows in the middle of the night.

"Dad," Ronny said, "Why don't you let me? Let me do it tomorrow when it's light."

You'll kill yourself, man, he thought but didn't say. He shrugged, looked at his father and hoped that this would end quickly, that it wouldn't require much of an argument.

"That's a waste, Ronny. Waste of a night."

His father squinted in at him, made his hand a visor to see into the room past the reflection. Ronny hadn't known what to do. It was like the night he'd come home from work late to find his father on the front porch, just sitting there on the steps in a daze, mumbling to himself, something about a conference in Tucson, both socks on but only one shoe.

The room had grown cold with the window open. His father's head was still pressed against the glass, and he was explaining something.

"In case I sell the house," he was saying, "the windows should be clean for when the people come."

Ronny had talked his father down from the ladder, taken his elbow and led him inside. When he went back later to return the ladder to the shed, he looked up at the sky as he unsteepled the thing, expecting something brighter than a dim thread of moon barely pulling through the gauze.

When Ronny rang the doorbell every evening. When Viv answered the door; when he saw her standing there, shy in her ill-fitting clothes, her hair pulled back so a few strands fell over her eyes, but her neck—you could see the back of her neck just below her earlobes where normally her long choppy hair, the hair she cut herself with the kitchen scissors, would hide it. When he saw her there in the doorway, every night, when she stood there on the threshold, he felt a palpable, urgent trepidation that this time she wouldn't lower her eyes as she moved to let him in. Each time she might hesitate, change her mind, tell him to go away.

For Ronny, everything hinged on the seconds that composed his nightly arrival. He needed her to appear in the doorway and let him in; she needed something, he could tell, and maybe from him, but who knew what it was. He'd told her all of it—most of it—everything about Pete and the fires and his general fucking misery. But what he knew about her he could, basically, count on one hand. Between the Doctor and Vivian, between the new job and the nights he spent with her, there wasn't all that much time for him to get into trouble anymore. He was laying kind of low. Which was a relief because—he hadn't admitted this to himself yet—but it was a close call with the fire outside Concrete Jungle. Way too close.

Ronny nudged the Dasher into a spot near the park, on the opposite side of the street from the hospital deck. He tried to avoid the parking deck as much as possible. If he parked on the street, it was only a five-minute walk to the Doctor's lab and he felt less like a patient or a visitor. The university hospital was too far out to walk from his father's place so he'd started taking the old Dasher again, the car he'd shared with Pete all through high school.

It was strange to drive it now because he felt he should be on his way to his first girlfriend's house every time he got behind the wheel. The last time he'd seen Evvy would have been Pete's funeral. They hadn't talked. He'd been surprised to see her, though. And now she was in Denver or some place. Once since the funeral he'd seen her mother, sometime last year—actually, he remembered, he'd seen her at the airport when he'd been moving out to his mother's during the divorce; that was when she'd told him Evvy was in Colorado. That's right. He smoked as he walked, thinking how he'd told Evvy's mother he was going to Russia, hoping the news would make it back to Evvy. If just for a second that got the image of a different Ronny in her head: of him at the airport, leaving . . . maybe he'd said Romania. She'd hugged him. Ronny had felt the stiff cotton of her shirt when he ducked his chin, leaned down to help her reach, he was so much taller. Evvy's mother could have watched him walking across the airport to his imaginary gate, probably had watched him, so he'd gone all the way around to the international counters just in case she did.

He flicked his cigarette into the ashtray near the door and muttered hello to the other smokers gathered on break, cigarettes and Styrofoam coffee cups in their hands.

Up the stairs he thought about how odd, how awful it was to be back in town after everything. And how awful that people who knew him, knew Pete and his whole family and all of it, like Evvy's mother, were probably still in town, too, but now it was a different geography, and the worlds they existed in were strictly removed from each other's, which was obvious in a town like this. Of course, Ronny was hardly around to run into people. But with a town that went on for barely twenty miles in any direction, you kind of knew that everyone you used to know who hadn't left already was somewhere nearby. Which, Ronny thought, made it that much more incomprehensible—he'd reached the Doctor's lab, and was sifting through his keys—where Paul had gone without anyone knowing how or where or why. He turned the key in the lock and felt the door give.

The Doctor was speaking German. It was guttural, a forest in the throat. The Doctor, phone hooked on his shoulder, pulled feathers from a bird's wing and continued to speak. *Junge, flügel, zunächst.* The wing was emerald green, dark enough to appear black until you got up close and saw how the green splints of wingtip shimmered under the bright bulb. The wing was no longer attached to its bird. Feather by feather Ronny watched the Doctor's forceps pluck, and he realized he'd never wondered what the Doctor did in lab. Since Ronny made sure the Doctor wasn't there when he cleaned, conversation between them had barely been required. He'd never had to think of anything to ask. Ronny started to the back of the room as the Doctor hung up the phone.

"Ron," the Doctor said, motioning him over to the table.

The Doctor placed another feather on the dish and set the forceps down.

"Sir?" He waited, leaned over to get a better look at the sparsely feathered wing, saying, "What are the names—*ulna, radius*—" Ronny had to think a minute, "Or no it's *humerus, ulna, radius*? I don't know, guess I've forgotten all that stuff, it's been a hundred years."

He had no idea what else to say or what was expected of him.

"What stuff is that? You've forgotten what stuff?"

Ronny glanced up from the wing to see that the Doctor was staring at him.

"I meant, just bird stuff," Ronny said, "terminology, taxonomy."

The Doctor didn't say anything else so Ronny shrugged.

"It's nothing. I mean, I went to camp, I used to go to this camp every summer, for nature, bird watching and hiking and stuff, a few years in a row I went. It was kind of for kids who couldn't get into soccer camp or anything better, but—" he shrugged again "—it was all right."

The Doctor was waiting for something. Ronny wished he would stop staring at him, though, and started rambling, nervous in the Doctor's hyper-attentive silence.

"My brother always had this thing he did," Ronny went on, "competitive cycling, and my parents really wanted me to have something that was, you know, my own interest, whatever. Long time ago."

Ronny jangled his set of keys hand to hand. That big silver ring never warmed to the touch no matter how long he held it. It seemed like he should get back to it. Get the mop from the closet, find the replacement bulbs. When he shifted his weight the Doctor noticed and leaned forward slightly, uncapped a pen with his thumb.

"Ron," he said finally. "I know that—well, put it this way, shall we."

He paused. He wasn't sure how long it would take for the information to sink in. Not too terribly long, he hoped.

"Let me say," he started again, "that I have been *informed* of certain things. For instance—"

Ronny was trying not to let his aggravation show. Until that afternoon, the Doctor had seemed dismissive, arrogant, aloof. He'd seemed stoic, preoccupied with important business. Intense, maybe, but in a way that had nothing to do with Ronny. Whatever he was on about now, Ronny wasn't in the mood for it.

"I know about your brother," he went on, "Pete, your brother—I know about him, a fair amount, but don't worry, you have no cause to be—"

"Why?" Ronny interrupted. "What does Pete have to do with anything?"

"—as I was telling you, you have no cause for alarm, but I do need to inform you that I know about your past, to a certain degree which I imagine will surprise you. Put it this way, Ron: I know you've been in some trouble, and that your family has had a tough time of it."

"What is . . . what're you trying to tell me?"

Ronny waited, not knowing where to look or what to think. How'd he know Pete's name, or anything about Pete? He searched for any memory of conversation, a time when he might have given any information, but forget it, he couldn't have, the Doctor had hardly spoken to him since their initial introduction weeks ago. He felt strange (was this tunnel vision, was he dehydrated, was he dizzy) and distracted by the Doctor's voice. He wanted a cigarette.

The Doctor continued, "I didn't know about camp, however, but it is an excellent thing for me to hear, Ron. An excellent confirmation."

"Ah," Ronny said, "confirmation for what? What?" His voice was louder than he meant it to be, but he was getting angry. He felt dumb for being confused; he felt pranked. Felt like an asshole. "What's going on?"

The Doctor considered Ronny before he continued.

"Ron," he said, folding his arms over his chest, "it's simple. You fit the profile. You are . . . between engagements, uncommitted. You have been in trouble with the law, so you could benefit from a steady, reputable opportunity—think of it as an internship. You are, if you don't mind my saying, in need of practical guidance. You've been coasting, you have too much time on your hands, certainly, and too much time, especially, for a person such as yourself, wouldn't you agree?"

Ronny stood there, not sure what he was hearing yet.

"As a matter of course, I don't condone illegal behavior," the Doctor went on, "but it does suggest something about your personality, your character, that I find interesting and rather useful for my purposes because it suggests you are a risk taker—and I find myself in the position of requiring . . . critical assistance from . . . a person who is willing to assist me somewhat . . . unconventionally."

"What the hell do you think you know, what do you—what are you saying?"

He'd been lured here, to the lab, and backed against the wall and hadn't seen any of it coming. What a fucking custodial ruse—what a tight fucking ship. Here he was being interrogated about his family, and what was the setup, what was the point of any of it—and who the fuck was this guy?

"Ron, understand, I need someone who acts on his impulses for better or worse. Your background—well, as unlikely as it might sound, is ideal. If you are prepared—are you? Are you prepared for this amount of responsibility?"

Ronny was not prepared. He put the keys on the table and put his hands in his janitor pockets.

"Wait," he said, struggling to keep his voice normal, "wait a minute, what the fuck is going on? You want me to do something and you used this job to get me here, and somehow you know about my family, I haven't figured out how, and you expect me to go along with something that sounds crazy, just for fuck's sake?"

He was fucking arrogant, this man, Ronny thought—that he could do whatever he wanted without anyone's objection—and how did he know this shit—

"How the fuck do you know about Pete?" he said.

His anger was on the verge of grief, which made him angrier, and he wasn't much of a fighter, so he didn't know what to do with the heat that was welling up in his fist. He gripped the table with his other hand. He didn't really want to punch this man; that would be depressing, like punching somebody's grandfather.

"You're the right man, Ron, I have confidence in your abilities. It hardly matters how I know," he said calmly, taking his glasses off, rubbing at one of the lenses with his sleeve, putting them back on.

"How the fuck do you know? Tell me."

The Doctor raised his eyebrows at Ronny's reaction.

"Ron, forget it, do yourself a favor, take my offer, Son."

"Or what?"

"Because you want to make something of your small life, presumably, am I wrong?" The Doctor's voice took on a hard edge, "No, of course I'm not, because that's all anybody can hope for. You're stuck in this town, this town has nothing to offer you—you don't even have your GED—you're going nowhere, if I may, and your mother's left you to take care of a very—troubled—man—"

Ronny pounded the table and some test tubes clanked against each other in the rack. He couldn't suppress his fury another second.

"Tell me," he said.

He had to get out of there. He shifted his weight, backed away from the table a couple steps. At this movement, at his slightest retreat, the Doctor relented. He sighed and said, "Your father's friend, Ron. He works in east third. He knew I was in the market for an assistant and made your case. I suppose he and your father go back some years, don't they?"

Ronny shrugged. This was fucked up. Of course people talked. Especially about other people's shitty lives.

"Listen, I'm sorry, but I don't get what you want me to do, here. What am I here for—and why me? Why the hell choose me if I'm such a disaster."

The Doctor took the time to smooth his tie flat against his shirt before he spoke, attempting to mask his exasperation.

"I want you to help me. As I told you, I believe you're right for this. I do not believe you would choose to polish the floors if given a choice between doing so and working with me, but—" he coughed, or cleared his throat "—correct me if I'm wrong."

Ronny knew the trap. He didn't care for his custodial duties much more than he cared for Concrete Jungle. He could deal with the push broom. He could deal with the washer on the leaky faucet in the restroom down the hall. But the ruse of sanitation and the Doctor and his top secret knowledge—he was not prepared to deal with such bullshit wizardry.

The Doctor kept talking. "As for why I've chosen you, Ron, singled you out, it's simple. You're impulsive. Your rash decision-making, as you may know, is a potential marker for a chronic cycle of criminal activity."

He paused to let that sink in.

"Unfortunately for you," he went on, "that compulsive tendency most likely will manifest in dangerous choices throughout your lifetime—if you continue to be unfocused, I should add. Fortunately for me, only a compulsive person with destructive behavior patterns would be willing to help me do what needs to be done, and you've already made some fairly serious mistakes."

Ronny felt as if he'd been punched. Here was a stranger telling him he was doomed and might as well cut his losses. Before he could say anything, the door opened and a doctor Ronny recognized vaguely, maybe from his cigarette breaks in the hospital-land park, strode into the room. One of the younger interns, bolder in his attempts to look suave than the other doctors Ronny had run into, a lumpy silver chain cabled around his neck.

"Excuse me, Doctor, sorry to interrupt," he paused, glancing at Ronny in his gray coveralls.

"Just wanted to drop off these files—you'll need them for the hearing. Make sure you fill out the forms."

And he tossed the folder down hard on the lab table, a force that caused a slight breeze to flap at the Doctor's tie.

"Well Ben, with all due respect," the Doctor cleared his throat, "Forms won't be necessary, I—"

The young doctor cut him off.

"If you think the Board will be pleased, Doctor—respectfully—you're wrong. That's protocol, and while that doesn't necessarily affect your actions around here, you should take this seriously."

He'd emphasized the word *respectfully* and sounded sarcastic, already halfway out the door but turning back into the room, looking first at Ronny then at the Doctor before he said, "Pardon the interruption. See you at the meeting."

He let the door slam.

Ronny waited for the Doctor to explain but he didn't. He shrugged, shuffling quickly through the files, closed the folder and dropped it in the trash can, walking back across the room to face Ronny again.

"Hearing?" Ronny said.

The Doctor shook his head.

"It's nothing; nothing worthwhile, anyway. But it does highlight the significance of this, and I need you to listen, Ron. I apologize if you feel—blindsided by all that I have revealed to you today. Of course you do."

He had a hard time meeting Ronny's eyes, but he went on.

"I'm asking for your help on something extraordinary, not

run-of-the-mill, not easy, nothing anyone around here could fathom at his most brilliant."

He shook his head, getting ready to give up on Ronny, probably, for being as obtuse as the rest of them.

"Why should I listen to whatever you're talking about here and not just—take off?" Ronny said.

The Doctor folded his arms across his chest, rocked back on his heels.

"Go back to your ordinary life, nothing changes. Stay in town, hold down some jobs, maybe go back to school, night classes, meet someone and get married, one day start a family, settle down, same as everyone. Fine, fine, great. But if you choose to assist me, Ron, you will become an integral part of a new history. That is not a gift to turn down with less than proper consideration."

Ronny met his eyes and quickly glanced away again; he had started to feel sorry for the Doctor, who despite his ego and his massive intellect was desperate enough to beg the help of a burnout who set fires.

"I need to know what you plan to do before I divulge further, however. These matters are critical, or there would be no need for any of this."

He gestured vaguely with both hands at the workbenches, the cabinets with their rows of glove boxes and flasks, the carts labeled *Room 504C DO NOT REMOVE*.

Ronny felt stranded. The problem was, when it came down to it—and it was a thing that caused a variety of sadness as depressing as it was liberating—when it came down to it, the problem was, it was true that he had nothing to lose. The Doctor was right about that. He had nothing to lose, he had nothing to risk. He had nothing. It was to this nothing he would return.

"Okay," he muttered. He shrugged as he nodded. He shrugged as he resigned.

"Tell me what it is."

From a small adjoining room the Doctor carried forth a box with a lid and set it on the table. It was a box with a system: metallic panels, ventilation portals, a heat lamp. The Doctor opened the lid and inside three baby birds huddled in a nesting box, eyes almost open.

"It's genius," the Doctor said. "The wing. We're building the human wing."

Ronny waited, staring at the birds in the box, and the Doctor said, "Yes, you heard correctly, I am designing a wing for humans. It is the time to do this, but it is not—*permissible,* according to the Board, the ethics committee, so you can understand why, as I mentioned, we adhere to a strict contract of confidentiality starting now."

The Doctor looked at Ronny over the top of his glasses, signaling that it was his chance to ask questions.

"What—do you mean, exactly, you're saying people who want . . . wings—"

The Doctor folded his arms and leaned forward to address Ronny directly.

"—and you are serious—this is serious?" Ronny said.

"I am less serious about all that I have known and done, Ron. Don't repeat that. My life's work has amounted to helping people tremendously during their—sometimes dire—misfortunes, and for that I am proud, profoundly, of course—but *this*—what I have planned, Ron—" He lowered his voice, straining to whisper loud enough, and went on, "—is the crowning achievement, a *reconception* of the human form! As the human form has never before been permitted to be reconceived."

He paused then, and said, "Yes, Ron. This is serious work. Now, if you agree to the assignment, you will help with research and essential mechanics. Obviously, there is funding to pay a full-time custodian. Officially, that will remain as the purpose for your employment, as far as Administration goes."

The Doctor tapped the incubator.

"But everything—every *shred* of information you collect as my assistant—stays in this room, yes? You can do this? Shouldn't be the hardest thing you've ever done."

Ronny studied the Doctor. He wore an orange tie and dress shirt that afternoon, not scrubs or a coat. He had a body that was worn out from anticipating greatness; during their conversation, his shoulders had slumped a little lower each time he tried to convince Ronny to stay, each time Ronny demanded information he didn't want to give.

The Doctor ushered Ronny to the room at the back of the lab. He had lined up feathers across the table, building an outline of a wing minus the bone structure. The wing, feathers removed, arced pale in a tin lid under a lamp. It reminded Ronny of his own naked rib cage and the room felt even smaller. Ronny nodded, and the Doctor offered his hand's forceful grip to make their partnership official.

The Doctor looked at his watch. "Okay, I am late now," he said, "What I need for you to do—keep your uniform—"

He walked over to his desk and gathered a stack of papers and medical journals and ornithological journals, thumped it down on the table in front of Ronny, saying, "Start with this. Read and take notes, as applicable—bone density, feather properties, structural dimensions, aerodynamics, innovative trials—read it all. And I will see you tomorrow. Any questions—I will see you tomorrow."

And the Doctor was gone, pulling the door shut behind him.

Ronny looked at the stack in front of him. Holy crap. *Wings* for Christ's sake. This was fucked up. How could this be real—was the Doctor out of his mind—what the hell was going on?

But he sat down at a lab stool anyway and reached for the first paper, glancing at the title. *Skeletal differences between bats (Chiroptera) and birds (Neognathae).* All right, he thought. Here goes.

Now that he was invested, Ronny started showing up to work earlier. It was easier than he'd figured to maintain his janitorial charade, as long as he made the typical rounds with tools in hand and unlocked/relocked a couple doors every few hours. He still checked in downstairs with the rest of the maintenance crew every day, and he still got called down to fix a leaky valve or, more rarely, the printer in the closet-sized office where the payroll admin was temporarily installed. And as long as he put in those typical task-oriented appearances, he could spend most of his shift hours catching up on his reading.

He even had books on sculpture artists—for weeks he studied the books on the flying machines Panamarenko made, charting in a big spreadsheet the adaptations for every obvious structural innovation. There were versions of Icarus with wheels and long feather-planks, and who knew if they could manufacture flight—they looked capable and impressive and he spent hours scrutinizing the mechanics of each Raven or Rucksack contraption. He understood the Doctor's fascination though he still thought the plan was insane (who on earth would elect to have gigantic wings grafted into his body, fused with his bones, permanently implanted?) but the fundamental, basic scheme, he got that, and he appreciated the magnitude of the theory, which was almost too colossal to fathom.

But as the weeks passed and his research progressed, Ronny grew more and more convinced. It wasn't impossible—it was like anything else: it would happen systematically, in a series of progressions put incrementally in place. And it might be grotesque—yeah, he could see that, grafting new appendages onto an ordinary form, a normal body, was grotesque and sci-fi and a thousand other things—but wasn't it also magnificent? Fuck, it was mostly magnificent, Ronny thought, and he was in no position to judge. Sure, he was desperate to realign his trajectory, to reorganize it beyond the supply closet, of course. What was the ultimate trajectory, if not flight?

OCTOBER 11, 1989

The morning rush had ended, the place empty again except for the delivery guy loading in the weekend supply of milk and creamer. Vivian began wiping down the counter, circular sweeps across the Formica that erased the coffee rings and drips of syrup. There was no sound at all and then there was an eruption of sharp bright heat on the back of her neck as the weight of it, the cold hot heat of it, pushed her hard to the floor, the steel O snubnose weight that pinned her down to concrete, an emergency of motion, a deadly unlifting, a gloved hand muzzling her mouth, his breath hot in her ear, *shut up bitch shut the fuck up don't move.*

Having been to the carnival. Having stood in line and waited her turn, and handed over three dollars for what the hawker promised was guaranteed whale-tooth scrimshaw—it was too cheap, it had no heft—Vivian gave up.

She preferred the off season, because in the off-season there was no notion that she might find Seth just by milling the fairgrounds, any fairgrounds. It would never cross her mind. Watching the performers weave in and out of the crowd, clad in sequin vests and painted faces, you couldn't miss the mimes or jugglers or contortionists. They always drew the biggest group of onlookers, unless there was a sideshow tent that promised less familiar attractions, like Lucky the Sword Swallower or the woman who ate pennies. This was more like a small town celebration with a cakewalk and pig races and booths rented out where you could toss pies, or guess the fat man's weight, or watch a woman in a headscarf paint your name with a single horsehair on a grain of rice, then loop it on a string around your neck. There was no mime, which meant no Seth. The juggler wasn't very good, but Vivian put two dollars in the dirty hat tipped in the dust anyway. She should've known it wouldn't be the right kind of carnival, but she'd gone because she'd thought it might make her feel closer to her brother, wherever he was. It didn't. Ronny had warned her when she'd mentioned it. He'd laughed, "It's like if the Rotary Club threw a picnic and rented a clown. It's not like going to Coney Island. It's the Rotary Club members and their housewives who bake quiche." Vivian hadn't told him why she wanted to go. Besides, he was right. She felt for the tooth in her satchel and rubbed the polished ridge of it with her thumb.

When she got back to Helen's house she checked the mail. Bills, an envelope from Helen, a discount consumer electronics catalog, a grocery circular. As she flipped through the stack, sifting out the junk mail, an envelope fell to the floor. She bent down for it, and saw the name. Paul _____. She paused. Mail addressed to Paul continued to arrive, of course, because the capitalist empire didn't know he was a missing person and therefore not currently in the market for credit cards or refinanced mortgages. But this looked like an actual letter, not junk, and it appeared to have been sent months ago—it was postmarked May, which was what, six months ago now—plus there was no return address. Just a few illegible cancellations, no good clues. She considered opening it and examined the packet, gauging the job: soft corners, kind of dirty, thicker than a single trifold sheet. She propped the letter on the mantle, separate from the rest of the mail, and decided she would wait.

The day Ronny located and bought a plastic replica of a common kestrel to see how its hollow bones crisscrossed small trusses of reinforcement was the same day the Doctor explained the procedure. He'd just hung up with the auctioneer when the Doctor arrived with an attaché case.

"In here—" the Doctor said, once the door was closed, "—in here is the pattern. Which means what comes next requires construction, which requires an apprentice, a volunteer, a—test subject, Ron. Right?"

Was he supposed to agree to something? Ronny wasn't sure what he'd been asked. Instead of answering, he told the Doctor about the kestrel model he'd tracked down.

"They're sending it out Wednesday so it should get here by Friday—sounds like it's in really good condition—"

The Doctor nodded impatiently and started again.

"That's all fine, I'm sure. What I'm asking here, Ron, is for you to consider lending your expertise and—enthusiasm—to the project in a special capacity—a specialized capacity. It would mean, basically, committing more than you can comprehend right now, but the resulting greatness, trust me, is inevitable, and to claim a part in such an achievement, I'm sure you'd agree, there's no argument, it would be a massive and certainly spectacular, certainly historical, thing to claim."

"You mean test subject, then," Ronny said.

He felt confused by the new development but also slightly—and despite his immediate misgivings—proud at being singled out.

"I would be the test subject, and—"

The Doctor interrupted, "Ron. Let me be clear: you'd be the first to test the prototype. You'd be instrumental in the most crucial phase, if you're willing, this is—no small thing, what I'm proposing."

"So I'd actually get these, the prototype, put on me, have them attached . . . ," Ronny said, "Well, wow, I don't know, I need to—think about it."

The Doctor nodded, "Certainly."

Ronny nodded too, out of politeness, but he was thinking what the fucking hell man, what the hell—the Doctor wanted him inside the experiment.

When Ronny got home from work that night, he thought the house seemed dark, but besides the mail still stacked in the box, nothing else was out of place. He headed to the kitchen, tossing coupons for the mechanic and credit card statements on the table, looking for sandwich bread. Thunder in the distance, and a steady rain that hammered the roof, the back deck, the grill. Both cars were in the drive so his father hadn't taken off. There was no sign that he'd been downstairs that day. No spread-open newspaper, no recycling out on the counter, no glass in the sink. The back of the couch was as much of the den as he could see from there—its copper floral slipcover and the shell of the table lamp next to it, the point of its pleated shade.

Ronny made another sandwich and went upstairs where he found his father in his old room, Ronny's old room, sitting at the desk, staring out the window. He couldn't see anything out there, with the rain sheeting down in the dark. Ronny stood by the desk and put the plate down in front of his father. His father didn't acknowledge his entrance right away, and when he eventually turned around Ronny wasn't sure he heard him correctly when he spoke.

"We got a call today. Your mother called to let us know, she's getting married. She wanted to tell you herself, but . . ."

Ronny didn't have anything to say. He stared at the sandwich. He'd had to use the heel for one side, and it seemed like a grim meal to deliver now that he was looking at it.

"Well," he said, when he realized he hadn't answered.

"Why would she?" his father said.

Ronny looked away. The man sitting at his small plywood desk was aged by that news, just from hearing it. He looked like he'd spent a lifetime shrugging things off and reaching for the same threadbare sweater, resigned to any number of unnamable, tedious concessions. Of course she wasn't coming back.

"Did she say anything else?"

Ronny stared at his feet, at the split rubber of his shoe.

"I don't know," his father said, "Why she would do that?"

Ronny had to get out of there.

"Well," he said again, "I'm sorry that—she called, that . . ."

It wasn't what he meant. He was sorry the news surprised his father, sorry that he'd expected things to work out differently, that this was one more ending. But his father wasn't listening anyway, his back slumped in Ronny's ancient, too-small chair, his elbows propped painfully on the desk. He fidgeted with the gold watch on his wrist, studying the time and staring at the plate in front of him, tracing its edge absentmindedly with his thumb. Then he picked up the plate and threw it at the wall. It cracked in half and dropped the sandwich to the carpet, an unappealing scatter of limp bread. Ronny watched him for a few minutes, surprised at his father's aggression. He didn't know if he should clean up the mess, and when he started to bend down to collect the plate pieces, his father said, "No, Ron, don't."

Ronny nodded and said, "I just—remembered that I have to go, pick up my last paycheck tonight."

"Hmm?" His father wasn't listening.

"Yeah, from the Jungle. They still have it, I'm going to go . . . pick it up."

"I guess so," his father said.

"Okay, I guess so," Ronny said.

Ronny backed out of the room, hurried down the stairs and headed straight out to his car. He sat inside with the heat blasting, letting the rain split the windshield into thousands of tiny oceans while he made up his mind. Fuck. There wasn't anything left that hadn't ended. He had nothing to lose. Not one dumb thing. He had no reason not to help the Doctor. Why shouldn't he do it? It sounded crazy, sure. But if it gave him a purpose—a purpose unlike anybody else's, a singular aim, an historically important, surgical masterpiece of a purpose—well, what else was there for him to do? End up miserable and resigned at fifty-seven, like his father, never even having managed to move out of town? To have the choice to do something off the charts, something that would rearrange a fundamental aspect of humanity—the Doctor's mission was persuasive. To solve one small sadness. Ronny could choose. He put the car in reverse, and snapped on the lights. Not going anywhere, exactly, but getting as far away as he could from that room.

NOVEMBER 16, 1989

From the *New Settlement of 1922 Log of Storms and Catastrophic Emergencies (1922-1928)*, p. 34:

Though the forecast predicted accurately the rain totals, the rate of saturation and the speed at which the winds gusted were grossly underestimated. The three days of steady rain, flooding on the plains, and sustained storm-force winds caused a "Gray out" and came to be known from the Spring of 1924 on as the Great Deer Lake Flood.* Thirty people perished. Ten of these victims were never identified. The twenty known victims are hereby registered by the Beacon Temple as: Robert Causey; Olivia Daniels; Anabella Edmonson; Fitzwilliam Ernsthauser; Percy Fanwell; Samuel E. Fraser; Icabod Frederick; Vivian M. Foster; Monty Cardon Heath; Loretta B. Henry; Sylvia Hester; Nora Holt; Ruth L. Messer; Padraic Nathaniel; Ralph D. Nelson; Henrietta Parson; Tomas Roe; Katya Ross; Charles Westen; Miranda "Milly" White. *See also <u>Weather</u>, <u>Deer Lake Region</u>, <u>Notable Drownings</u>.

Maybe she was meant for another century. Fainting gloves, Finnish lachrymatory bottles, horsehair kerchiefs. An assassin in the trunk room. The station in Argentina, heavy scent of perfume in the train car. Lilacs. A lifetime of mourning the heist.

"Vivian." Someone was saying *Vivian, Vivian.*

"Hey, sleepyhead," he said, resting his hand on her shoulder.

The room was bright. There was a movie on. Peter Sellers flickered on the television. Peter Sellers holding a suitcase.

"What," she said. "I'm awake."

"You didn't hear my question."

Ronny turned the sound down until the dialogue barely registered.

"What?" she said. Her eyes were closed.

"I said, have you ever thought about plastic surgery? I mean, what do you think about it, if you have thought about it, what's your opinion?"

Vivian kept her eyes closed. He was waiting. "What?" She started. "Do you mean because you wish—"

Suddenly she thought he meant her breasts were too small. She shook her head without meeting his eyes and her face burned; she didn't finish the question.

"No, stop," Ronny reached over and cupped her chin, "No Vivian. That's not what I meant, stop."

He pulled at her wrist to get her to look him in the face.

"I'm sorry," he said, "Okay? That's not what I meant."

He let go and stood, walked to the other side of the room. For a minute he paced and then stopped, looking out the window in the direction of his father's house.

"No, listen, I meant, what if they could do anything to a person that you could possibly want, you know, even if it was this really extreme, radical thing? What do you think about that?"

"I don't know," Vivian shrugged, "Like what?"

All she could think of was a bifurcated tongue because she'd met a man once with the tongue of a snake.

"Say you could change something about yourself in some extreme— way."

He turned back to her to see if she was thinking it over. He had a beard by then; he already looked older than when she'd first met him.

He looked like a rogue voyager setting out for the hinterlands, earnest and compelled to set forth and make a miraculous discovery.

"I don't know," she said, "I can't picture it."

She couldn't. She hated scalpels.

Ronny reached for his jacket, slung over the armchair, and checked his cigarettes: three left.

"Anything, though. Just anything. If you could—I mean, *because* you could technically do this procedure, whatever it was, should you? You want it, it's possible, is there any reason why not, why you wouldn't do it? Shouldn't do it?"

"You want me to say something, something specific, but I don't know what. Why? What is it?"

Ronny didn't say anything.

He ran his hand through his hair, making it stand out from his head even more than usual. She thought of a trawler. She thought of the ocean. Vivian squinted at him. She was so tired she'd forgotten to tell him about the letter. It was still on the mantle in the other room.

"What about—" Ronny took out a cigarette, rested it on the edge of the bookcase. "Did you ever want wings?"

His lighter was in his jacket pocket.

Vivian looked at him, unimpressed with whatever he was trying to establish. He was getting nowhere.

"Hold on," Ronny said, shrugged the jacket on, feeling at the pockets, "I want to show you something."

The books were in his car, parked down the block at his father's house.

After he left, Vivian surveyed the room: the glasses they drank from, the ashtray that was now full of ashes, the *Seven Day Detox* book Ronny had taken from the shelf and left tented on the floor. They were playing house. They were forgetting their actual lives here, the constraints, the logistics. It had been ages since she'd called her mother.

A red light flashed on the phone. She'd missed a message. She pushed the button and a voice unwound into the room that she didn't recognize at first. There was background noise that made it harder to hear, voices or traffic or lite radio jazz.

"Hello? Hello, are you there to pick up? Hello? Vic—Vivian, hell*ooo*—"

Flustered, the caller dragged the word out and shouted into the machine. Helen, calling to tell her the check would be late. There was a freeze on one of the accounts, she should watch for it in the mail late next week, she was sorry, *so sorry*. But was she calling from a payphone? Helen sent Vivian a check every month, enough for groceries, and Vivian didn't pay rent to Helen, which made it possible to get by on very little if she was careful, and she was careful. Vivian hit rewind and erased the message. Why would she call from a payphone? She was dialing her mother when Ronny came back and dropped a stack of notebooks and folders on the couch as she counted. Four rings, five, six, seven rings—then a voice was saying *hello, hello,* but not her mother's voice—

"Yes?" Vivian said, "Hello?"

"Hello?" Not her mother, again, but how—had she gotten it *wrong*—she couldn't have, no, this was it—definitely, this was the right number—

"Yes?" It took her a few seconds to remember what to say. "Is Mrs. Foster there, please?"

There was a long pause while Vivian waited for the woman to return.

"I'm afraid—may I ask who this is?" The woman hesitated. Vivian realized she hadn't left the phone at all. She wasn't checking.

"This is, I'm Vivian." More silence. "I'm Vivian, her daughter. Who is this?"

"Oh, dear," the woman said, "dear, this is the neighbor, your mother's neighbor, I came to check when my husband— "

"What?"

Vivian's heart was already a racehorse in her throat and her collarbone felt hot and tighter as if she was shrinking bone by bone, as if her body was constricting, she had never felt so disgusted by her body, which had suddenly become a cage.

"What?"

The woman drew a breath and said, "My husband noticed the goat was out—the goat, he never strays this far, it's three miles out to our pasture. My husband saw the goat and we took him back home, and when my husband brought him back and I went inside—the door was unlocked and no one answered, your mother was—on the floor in the—I couldn't see at first but she was, maybe she fell, my husband called the ambulance, but they said she was already—she hadn't been breathing when they came, already they could tell by, they could tell—that she was, she wasn't—Would you like to take some time, would you like to discuss this later—if now is not—"

"No," Vivian said, even though she was having a hard time focusing on the conversation. There were gaps in her comprehension, as if her brain kept turning off after every few words the woman spoke so it sounded like: *Dear, I have to that we find any records of power of decisions and what dear it pains prearrangements and the social worker usually reserved I'm afraid, if there were would have preferred afraid . . .*

Vivian didn't know anything about arrangements or preferences. She didn't know anything, which meant she was off the hook in a way that left her feeling not wholly part of any of this. Another dimension removed.

The woman was trying to remain composed enough to talk. Vivian was excruciatingly aware of how terrible, how unfair it was to have to report the news that someone was suddenly dead, especially to a complete stranger, especially over the phone. It was ridiculous. It was horrible.

"I'm terribly sorry, terribly, dear. Vivian? You said your name was—"

"Yeah," Vivian mumbled. She felt behind her for the armchair and sat down. She couldn't think.

"Oh it's a lovely name, dear, it's—I'm sorry—well, I didn't know. My name is Betty Randall . . . well—I imagine you will be coming here, to take care of—would you take my phone number, Vivian, if you need anything at all, if we can help at all, I know you're not prepared right now but when you need something—I know it's a shock dear, let me give you the number."

Vivian just listened, didn't try to find a pen. "Okay, thank you," she said after a little while, to nobody. She sat there and listened to the phone drag into the dial tone until it disconnected and started beeping. Ronny tried to take the phone from her and hang up.

"Vivian," he said. "Vivian."

She had to keep her eyes closed. She couldn't breathe. She was in a cage   a cage a white word   white, white,   and she was suffocating, white, and it hurt, everything was hot white   pinpricks her scalp, her arms, the back of her knees stinging *white*   *white white   white   white.*

Vivian?

Ronny shook her, said *look at me* but she couldn't she couldn't she couldn't she couldn't she couldn't look couldn't think couldn't breathe.

"Vivian," Ronny said. "Stop. Vivian. What's wrong, what, Vivian?"

What   what   what   like a moving cage, like a jail, was she going crazy, was that the problem, because that was the manner you took with people who broke down, short short sentences and name repetition, like training a small animal any command. Vivian wasn't crying, it wasn't her sobbing that had gotten to Ronny, it was the cage she was in, just sitting there frozen, not making any sounds at all, not talking, not crying.

"What?" he said. "Please, *what?*"

Not moving, not even there anymore, not there, not anything, only white and white and hot.

White white

white

.

Vivian woke to a dark pocket of room. Ronny stirred—he'd fallen asleep propped up against the headboard—and reached over, gently brushed the hair from her forehead. She felt hot.

"Are you okay?" His voice was hoarse.

She tilted her head to see him; she had to look up. "Sorry," she mumbled.

"No," he said. "There's not, there's nothing to be, you know."

His hand rested lightly on the crown of her head. He wanted to smoke. Part of him wanted to leave.

"You didn't have to," she said. "You can leave."

"It's okay," he said, but she was already falling back to sleep.

When she woke again it was from a nightmare of water. A house pulled into the lake, brown and rusty water filling the rooms and rising quickly, swelling to the ceiling. Huddled on the roof she held a magic dog the size of a sandwich under her chin where he would be safe for a second, but the horizon was falling to pieces, and the water was reaching her ankles, her elbows, her throat—

She kicked at the heavy blanket; it would not budge. It wanted her to drown in that house with the very small dachshund.

She startled awake. She was hot, it was hot in the room, and where was Ronny; she sat up on her elbows. "Ronny?" She called out. "Ronny?"

The room was empty. Maybe he had left after all. It was still dark out. She couldn't tell if it was the darkness of night or morning.

There was a sound in the hallway and then Ronny was at the door, a glass of water in his hand. "Hey," he said, sitting at the edge of the bed, "I couldn't wake you up, it seemed like you were having a bad dream. I brought you some water."

She reached for the glass and gulped half of it down in one long swallow. The hammer of cold ached but it felt good and hefty.

"I was drowning," she said, "I couldn't save it. The roof was floating away. I was going to miss my plane."

Ronny stroked her arm, dragging his fingers from the inside of her wrist to her shoulder; she shivered at that light touch and felt grounded, back in her skin.

"I don't want to be left alone," she told him, "don't leave right now."

"No," he said, "I don't have to go."

In a minute he said, "Do you need anything, can I get you something?"

She shook her head. She curled her knees up to her chest and stayed like that, tucked into the covers and hiding her face. Black splotches drifted and raced behind her eyelids. She counted to twenty. It wouldn't stop. She moved the pillow and sat up again, concentrating on the mess of bedspread.

"Ronny," she said. She pulled at the blanket and worked a thread loose at the corner, ripping the seam a little. "Ronny, I have to go to Nebraska."

She waited for a minute and then she said, "My mother died."

"Jesus," he said, "Vivian, that was—the phone."

He thought about his own mother, how she'd called his father to tell them she was marrying that guy who owned the Italian restaurant, and he couldn't help it: he mostly wondered if she was still letting him borrow her car, having him drop her off at the bank before every shift. He hadn't spoken to her since he moved back. Now he felt guilty for not minding nor really noticing this lapse in communication.

"Viv, are you okay?" Ronny could tell she didn't want to talk and he wasn't sure how to get it right, how to be helpful or if he should back off, or—

What happened to Pete, when it happened, Ronny didn't want anything to do with the sympathy cards his teachers sent and the abrupt endings of conversations when he walked into rooms or past groups of people, neighbors, friends of Pete's or their parents. He wanted it fucking over. Not the way his father did, pretending nothing had happened, disproportionately pleased with everything, including, for example, his daily breakfast of generic Raisin Bran. Not like that. He didn't even mind the quiet, so much as he minded the pity and the gossip that roamed and circled against the quiet. He had gotten into a fight when Mannifred Harding had said something at just the right volume for Ronny to catch it, two lockers down. Mannifred the Man or Hard Man Harding had the perfect name for a guy of his bullish stature, a macho asshole rich guy, a joker who had a big square head and wore his hair shaved on the sides and in the back but long enough in the front so it flopped over his eyes and had to be constantly dealt with. What Mannifred the Man Harding said was, *Maybe now Pete's gone Ronny can be less of a loser, and maybe he should thank Pete for that.* It was true. Pete had been the more popular of the brothers, the more traditional jock, because though cycling might have been what he did on his own, basketball was what he played at school, and he was a good forward; cheerleaders wanted to cheer him to glory and jocks wanted him in all their jock clubs, at all their jock parties, parties Ronny was never invited to. None of which mattered anymore, but on that day the rage Ronny held against Hard Man and his friends, those real asshole fuckheads, could not be suppressed any longer, and that day Ronny punched Hard Man square in his face and smashed his cheekbone. Mannifred had not swung back, he'd said, because he felt sorry for him, *for the loser*, and Ronny got ISS but it didn't matter; he was on his way out soon enough. Hitting Mannifred had felt great, and necessary in the scheme of things, but all Ronny had wanted back then was to be left alone. Who would Vivian punch. Ronny had no idea.

When it was morning and time for Ronny to go to work, he made coffee and brought it to Vivian who sat up in bed. Who looked like she had not slept in a week. Who thanked Ronny for coming as if he'd been invited for a proper celebration and was the last straggling guest to leave and she was slightly embarrassed for him. Her hair fell across her face, a soft shadow, and the light through the window blinds split the room in thirds, light lighter lightest.

He stalled in the doorway, lighter. "Can I stop by tonight, then?"

"I might be packing," she said into the mug.

"Well, maybe you'll need help . . . with something." He let his words fall away from the room. He knew every minute that passed between them corresponded to another small retreat.

When his mother first left, Ronny and his father had both slept through it. She'd taken a cab in the middle of the night, or just before dawn; they never knew and never asked. Just fingered the postcard she had scrawled her note on, *Will call in a few days.* The one that had been taped to the refrigerator door: a souvenir from the Air and Space Museum. It was called INFLATING JOHN STEINER'S BALLOON, JUNE 18, 1857, ERIE, PA. Ronny remembered it. The first photograph of an American aircraft: a great globe of taffeta cloth and goldbeater's skin. Waist-coated gentlemen gathered at the base of the balloon, struggling to hold the tethers despite the stormy winds that bellowed and quivered to cast off and carry John Steiner away.

At noon Vivian made herself get out of bed, tired of not sleeping. She was stalling to avoid the obligatory system of events that getting out of bed would set into motion, a series of chores she dreaded. Packing, showering, dressing, calling Helen for permission to skip town. She thought it all out in a checklist, getting through each activity without having to dwell on any part of any process. She took off her clothes standing in the bathroom thinking *undress*. She turned the faucets and made them correspond to warmth thinking *water*. Standing under the water she thought *shampoo*. Done, she thought *towel*. She thought *dress, toothpaste, hairdryer, boots*. But she still needed a map, directions, cash. There was another thing: somehow she'd have to find Seth. She'd have to tell him the news, and she didn't have the first idea how to go about searching for him. Carnivals and circuses traveled, and state fairs might be regional, but if each region had its own operational season—was there a chief commander? Was there a head secretary of fairs and carnivals? Was there a bureau? An office with a fax machine? A PO Box? Her first impulse was to look in the phone book under State Fair.

At least she had her mother's address from when she had called the Agency of the State of Nebraska's Rural Outreach Program and gotten it, years ago, when she felt that, at the very least, she should know her mother's address. Because all along she had known this was a possibility, that her mother would die alone out there, in the middle of nowhere, but she'd never stopped to consider how it would actually happen, or what she would have to do when it happened, if it did. And now it had. It was horrifying, and inevitable, and that her mother had been alone at the end—it seemed like the signal of a pathetic, failed life. She felt sick, like her breathing was constricted, like she needed to open a window, like she was going to throw up.

She needed to concentrate on the logistics and she needed to hold it together. She needed to pack. She needed to leave. She would have to call Helen but there was no way to explain without upsetting her. She would lie. She would manufacture something joyful and important. She needed to think. She was in the kitchen. She was swallowing a wrist-wide shot of bourbon. She was warmer and she was not hungry. She swallowed the bourbon and her throat burned and when she had finished her throat felt gently scorched, gentle like a dull knife lodged in the back of her throat, steady and steady and steady and pressing. She had to pack. She had to call Helen. She had to go.

She dialed Helen's number, relieved when the phone rang just twice before the prerecorded message came on. A machine (she pictured it) propped on a table in the butter-colored entryway of a condo in a gated community in Pensacola. She spoke quickly and cheerfully, said it's fine about the check and by the way her best friend had just gone into labor in a city about three hours north, and if Helen would permit a brief absence—just a brief celebratory absence—the less she said, she decided, the better. Hanging up, Vivian took her duffel bag and gathered what little there was to gather. In ten minutes she was packed.

She paced the room. She paced the hallway. She felt remarkably calm after the bourbon. Felt held fast to that hallway as she paced from the kitchen to the bedroom to the kitchen, thinking *how do you do this,* meaning: how do you find your missing brother who is mute, who is a mime, who is nowhere, to tell him your mother is dead.

Meaning: how do you get to Nebraska when your mother has died and the last time you saw her she was smuggling batteries she'd lifted from the gas station mini-mart into her suitcase, along with some clocks, the battery-operated can opener, cans of green beans with almonds and the shortwave radio.

Meaning: how do you live and live, and how do you live.

Ronny didn't know what to do. He sat on the hood of the Dasher and smoked, watching the neighbors' house, keeping his distance. The dark night was thick with cold and his breath clouded each exhalation like signals that gathered and rose up to the sky. One light upstairs, one light downstairs, he couldn't tell if Vivian had left yet or not. All day he had tried not to think about her, memorizing the measurements of second primary feathers and sixth primary feathers for the Doctor's prototype, R = *wing length from wing base to wing tip*; C = *wing chord* = *wing length as straight line from leading to trailing edge*. Aerodynamics. All afternoon Ronny jotted these notes and formulas to log alongside the model wing—*For bird, wing length* = *wrist joint to wing fold from bend of wing to longest primary feather*; F = *length of closed wing*; R = *length of wing*; Cm = *length of maximum chord*. He hadn't gotten to show her what he'd retrieved from his car the night before; she'd been on the phone when he came back in, so she knew nothing of this experiment, and now—he didn't know what his next move should be. He put his cigarette out, grinding the last glow of it into the bottom of his shoe.

He wasn't going inside. For the last week his father had taken to retiring to his office early to set up the miniature green plastic soldiers and stage battles based on a book about the Civil War he'd found in the attic. He made formations across his desk, along the windowsill and the closet shelf, formations that stretched down the ironing board, across the top of the television. Battalions, enemy lines, crossfire: he dropped them by the fistful and made exploding sounds with his closed mouth. Ronny could hear the wars playing out overhead every night after dinner as he shouldered on his coat and headed out the door.

That night Ronny hadn't bothered going inside, just pulled up and got out and sat on the hood of his car, figuring out what to do next. The fact was he knew hardly anything about Vivian: she came from out of nowhere to inhabit a stranger's house and made no show of having left the slightest attachment behind, as if she had no past. No best friend who wore the same size and stole the houndstooth coat Vivian had loaned her last winter; no ex-boyfriend whose name conjured a specific, reconsidered sadness that tugged at her mouth; no dumb jobs or misdemeanors; no family.

He'd been out there almost two hours by the time there was a sound down the street as a front door pulled open and then knocked closed, a sound that traveled faster in the cold. He jumped down and slowly headed out to the street, hesitating, so he'd meet her just as she was walking by and it could seem casual and convenient and acceptable, his interrupting her like that. He didn't want to interfere, but he had to: she was about to walk right past him into the night and disappear. She reached him there, in the frozen street, and stopped, shifting her duffel bag to the other shoulder.

"Hey," she said, looking off somewhere a little past him, not meeting his eyes.

"Is the closest bus station on King or Dolly?"

Ronny shook his head, "You can't walk, Vivian. Not this late."

"It's not even seven—"

"It's dark, so it's late enough, and it's at least twenty blocks."

He kicked at a branch that was frozen to the curb, splitting it loose. "No way," he said, "let me drop you off."

She didn't relent right away. They just stood there.

"Okay," she said finally, ducking her head, "All right, thanks."

She started to the Dasher and Ronny followed. The Dasher was slow to warm up and they sat without speaking for a few minutes before the vents pushed out burnt-smelling heat. Vivian wasn't wearing a proper coat, just a sweatshirt over some thick wool tights and a skirt—or dress, he couldn't tell—and boots, with a nubby orange ski cap pulled down to her eyes, a gray flannel scarf so long it looped around her neck twice then draped across her shoulders, and gloves frayed off at the knuckles. He hadn't noticed about the coat until he saw her fingers.

"Wait here, okay? I need to grab something first."

Ronny didn't give her a chance to answer, just jumped out and rushed to the house. Sneaking past the kitchen, he paused at a door in the back hallway. He opened the closet slowly and rummaged through the hangers for the castoffs, the vest of the suit his father got married in, Ronny's old track jacket, Pete's old winter coat which he folded over his arm, careful not to think about it. He made his way back to the front door and pulled it shut behind him, relieved to be outside. He carried Pete's coat down to the car (it was thick with a militaristic weight and vaguely musky, like dead leaves and copper) and saw right away how Vivian was gone.

He did a U-turn and headed in the direction of the station. She couldn't have gone far. And it wasn't long before he found her, just three or four blocks away. It was icy, she was underdressed, and the frozen bank where she walked was strewn with aluminum cans and broken hubcaps, which made it harder to walk quickly. When Ronny pulled up she was visibly relieved, out of breath, flushed and wiping her nose with the back of her glove.

"Sorry," she said. "I'm sorry, I couldn't wait, I have to get there, I'm already so late, I just—"

She started to say something else then stopped, shook her head. She got back in the car, shivering, cupped her hands to her mouth.

Ronny reached over, resting his hand briefly, barely, on her knee. Her skin was cold through the tights. He pulled the coat from the back seat and blanketed her lap.

"I'm sorry," she said again.

They drove west with the radio off, five minutes, and they crossed the tracks, long stretches of pitch black punctuated by a water tower, and then a cold storage unit, a couple of guys still hauling lockers into the back. A third guy hanging out up front, parked on the concrete steps, can in one hand, elbow on his knee. There was no spotlight rigged up above the drive and the bay of delivery doors, just the shallow fluorescence that flickered inside the unit and crept out to illuminate the immediate cusp of night shrouding the back door.

Not so far down from that they passed the Bar None Comfort Motel, which touted itself via busted marquee as "Just Like At Home," which actually it was not at all like. Not at all. It was like: if there was a group of salesmen buddies, say four of them, who'd gotten laid off because their branch of the trophy company was closing, and they went out drinking, and after a couple of hours, one of them announced to the others he had some coke, so they went to the Bar None to continue their party, and there two of them were, jostling outside the lobby near the bank of pay phones, aggressively bumming cigarettes and waiting for the escort to arrive. Bar None was down on its luck—it had been condemned and reopened twice—and it was the establishment nearest the bus station. And so, with less than a quarter block to go, Ronny said what he'd been thinking the whole way, as Vivian watched the scrapyard and the propane distribution plant and the gas station fall away in the side view mirror.

"Let me drive you there," he said.

She didn't stop looking out the window or answer right away. Eventually she said, "What do you mean." Not even like a question, not mildly curious, not politely interested in what he meant. They pulled into the parking lot but Ronny left the engine running and stayed far off to the edge, not anywhere near the passenger drop-off.

"How long does the bus to Nebraska take?" he said.

She shrugged, didn't say anything.

"I can drive you," he said, shaking his head, "It's not a big deal, it'll be faster than the bus, okay?" For a second he thought about work, about how he'd have to explain this to the Doctor, but he never thought about not going. He'd call the lab in the morning; so far he'd never had a sick day, had never even been late for a shift.

Vivian stared at him. Her eyes were sunken, underlined by dark circles, and her face was pale.

"You can't, though," she said, huddled under the tent of Pete's coat, her knees drawn up and her feet tucked under.

Ronny didn't know what to say. How could he explain, without sounding like a fucking idiot, the feeling he had that he'd never see her again if she got on that bus, and that he wasn't worried for her sake, but for his own? Fuck.

"Vivian," he said, "The bus takes longer. At least two hours."

He couldn't let her go.

"No," she said, "you can't help me."

"I won't help," he said, "I'll drive you wherever in Nebraska you need to go and I'll leave."

She didn't say anything. But she didn't make a move for the door either. Ronny put the car into first and pressed in the clutch. A quarter rolled down the dashboard at the shifting.

"Wait," Ronny said, desperate to convince her, "perfect, we'll use that. Heads is car, tails is bus."

Vivian leaned over to get the coin from its landing place at the tip of the floor mat. She palmed it, then held it out for Ronny to see.

"Okay," he said, "okay." He sighed, almost giddy with relief. "Let's go buy a map."

Sixty-three years ago, at the edge of a seaside town that boasted two pawn shops for every man, a small boy ducked into the sideshow at the annual fair against his father's strict warnings. The boy couldn't believe the kerosene mouth, the blue fire that should melt lips but instead was a flag saluting Behold and Surrender. And the carnie with his meatpacking hands shoveled the boy's coins into a slot marked Prix and pulled the curtain.

The boy could barely drag himself from the fire-eater's booth and into the curtained tent. Sliding onto a bench he waited impatiently, starting at each clatter or squawk; once or twice a chicken scurried in and circled the dirt floor for bits of corn cob. He raised his feet up, hugging his knees to his chest, fists sweaty, and just when he couldn't stand another second of this endless, urgent waiting, the screen swung open to reveal a large and gilded cage—a gilded monster of a cage—and inside the cage, a staggering thing:

A girl with wings.

At the snap of the barker's fingers the pedestal on which the girl stood began to slowly, slowly rotate.

From all angles the girl looked to the boy like a normal girl, ankles cuffed in lacy socks, her hair swept into ribbons and braids. But she was the palest human he had ever seen, wrists so white they seemed translucent, hair so blond it was clear. Two swan-sized wings sprouted from the blades of her shoulders, arcing magnificently into the air, silken feathers cursived into glorious structures that fluttered and trembled under the stares of the crowd.

He could not take his eyes away. Not albino. Not angel. Not bird. Not exactly human. No word for what she was.

NOVEMBER 30, 1989

When it happened it was not at all like she'd imagined. The platform below her swayed and rumbled for a long time, minutes, maybe seven or eight, before the cable must have righted, recalibrated the elevator's weight. By then she was crouched on the floor, trying to remember if she should stand back up or jump or lie down flat if the elevator started to fall. And then the box went dark, except for the emergency button on the operation panel, a little red knob. She waited for a long time in the silence. She had no idea how much time had passed. She drifted somewhere in the dark, imagining she was in southern Iceland, walking through the divotted farmland which was giving way to glacier in the distance. She was reaching the ice, stacked pristine and glassy into the sky; retreating from the coast, the black sands; she was climbing higher; she was almost there. She pushed the button and waited for a voice to cut through the static, to offer some direction.

If she wasn't so tired, Vivian probably wouldn't have given in so easily to Ronny's coin toss. But she was tired. She was exhausted. She was wasted. She closed her eyes and listened to the rush of the car's radiator and felt utterly cold, because even with that hot dry air pouring over her legs she couldn't get warm, she was chilled down to the bone where what was frozen was unreachable. With her eyes closed and no distractions, just immediate dark and hypnotic motoring, before she could snap out of it, she was remembering things: the dreary Thanksgiving afternoon, probably ten years ago, the furnace broken for days, hats and gloves and coats kept on inside. They were waiting for their mother to finish coloring her hair, smoking over the kitchen sink. When the egg timer rang, she bent her head to the faucet. Dinner was soda crackers and relish, dripped from jar to cracker with a fork. That night their mother flipped through the television's seven or eight stations for hours, an epic cycle of noise and light that filtered through the room in flashes. Vivian and Seth fell asleep on the couch, waiting for her to make up her mind about anything and decide on the rerun of M*A*S*H or *Dallas*.

Vivian opened her eyes to stop the old scenarios from creeping in with their shabby interiors and cold nights and gloved hands working rapidly to secure the hours shifting, shifting from the house. Now she was alone, absolutely; she was leaving nothing behind but a stranger's empty house. Seth was gone. Her mother was no longer at the other end of a stretched out wire. Ronny was there, but he didn't know the first thing about her and that's probably why he stayed. It was possible he thought he was saving her from something, protecting her, desperate for distraction from his life since Pete. She knew it was Pete's coat he'd brought her, though he hadn't said. It was how he went back for it, and how he carefully tucked it over her, even though there was already a sleeping bag in the back seat.

Vivian was tired but she was wide awake. The telephone poles and the treetops and the tips of weather vanes atlased the night sky and the outskirts felt vast. Every once in a while they'd pass a cluster of houses, a gas station, a strip mall and its deserted parking lot. By the time Ronny spoke, Vivian was already thinking how the year her mother quit leaving the house altogether was the year Seth stopped speaking completely, and

Vivian locked herself in her bedroom and studied maps of Newfoundland and Winnipeg and LA. Going, going, gone. Punched thumbtacks into the places she would visit, X'd off days as they passed. From then on when she ran into Seth in the hall or kitchen he waved or nodded hello instead of saying it.

"The other night, I wanted to tell you something," Ronny said.

He paused and looked over at her and looked at Pete's coat, "Do you remember what I said about plastic surgery and stuff, body modification? What your opinion was."

She nodded, hitching the coat over her knees.

"Well, you can't say anything to anyone, when I tell you this, okay, no matter what."

She looked at him, because who would she tell.

"I just need you to know," he said, "that you're not supposed to know."

She nodded.

"Okay," he said, and glanced over at her again. "I'm working for a doctor who is building human wings. Wings *for* humans."

Vivian stared at him and Ronny tried to tell her again.

"*Wings*—wings that can be surgically implanted into a person's body. Like real wings, huge and proportioned for flight, and permanent."

"For flying?" she said, "to fly with?"

"Yes. I'm not making this up."

"But," Viv said, "how does . . ."

"It's an experiment," Ronny said, "but it's real, yes. No shit. This doctor is building a pair of wings. I've got tons of papers, research and plans, dimensions drawn up on graphs, these insane reports and instructions, seriously, that's what I wanted to show you the other night."

Vivian pictured Ronny with wings. Tried to. Feathered, arcing masts that swept from his lower back all the way up to his shoulders: tufted, undeniable, spanning time.

"Are they feathered?" she said. "Human wings?"

She didn't even know if she'd heard him correctly. Were they talking about the same thing, because this was sounding absurd, and she was having a hard time concentrating.

"I don't think so, no. Feathers aren't necessary for flight, so . . . they're probably made out of something that resembles skin. PVC?"

They drove on for a few miles. Sparse flurries sparked on the windshield, brief crystals that melted as soon as they lit on the glass.

"I always thought you worked in an office. With other office people and office things," Vivian said after awhile.

"Actually I'm a janitor," Ronny said, "at the hospital. I have to wear a uniform while I'm there. Sometimes I fix the faucet that won't turn off in the bathroom."

He took a cigarette from the pack on the dashboard and pushed in the car lighter.

"Do you mind?"

She shook her head, rolling her window down a few inches, letting the cold in. It sharpened everything. When the lighter popped out, she held it up.

"Thanks," he said, exhaling out his window.

"Would you do it?" she asked.

Ronny shrugged, "I keep thinking, why not?" he said, "Why not? But I don't know. Would you?"

Vivian stared out the window, trying to picture it. How would it get mapped, the region of your brain that had to sense the wings? How would your brain distinguish between your arms and your wings? How heavy would they be: like a rucksack packed with flour, or like a floater, an incalculable lightness that lifted you forward aerodynamically, imperceptibly?

"What do you think?" Ronny said again.

Vivian looked at him. "I want to say yes. I want to say I would."

Fire was for burning. It was an energy his fingers itched over. It was a restlessness and an instinct. That was the only way he could explain it: a physical sensation that snuck up on him, came over him, rose up in him—one of these or all of these and all at once, a wave, a compulsion. That was the counselor's word, *compulsion*, and Ronny would give him that, but the rest of it he got wrong—the lame profile he showed to Ronny: a chart that fell out of one of his textbooks and divided up a colorful wheel like MALE 90%, and FEELINGS OF SADNESS/FEELINGS OF LONELINESS/ FEELINGS OF RAGE (INABILITY TO EXPRESS), and GAMBLER, and POSSIBLE LINK TO HYPOGLYCEMIA. It was bullshit. It was the worst pie chart Ronny had ever seen. The counselor threw the word pyromania around. Said Ronny must have been an irrational and self-destructive child; that he had *limited to no impulse control* and a criminal mind and that he lacked restraint.

He got it fucking wrong. Ronny had a compulsion, but that was it. There was no intent or deliberation, there was just striking the match, or holding the wheel of the lighter and crouching down to the dry grass patched along the fence of the tire factory. It was comforting, that small heat. The soft matchbook he kept in his shoe during track meets. It was just something he did, but he could *not* do it, too, no problem. Sometimes he just felt like something had to happen. He didn't want to hurt or de-stroy anything, though. He could smoke without burning anything down. Lighting a cigarette didn't make him want to set a tree on fire—although he had accidentally done that, once, the time he burned the boxes behind the 7-11. But he left buildings alone and if you asked him, lighting boxes didn't make him a criminal. That counselor was way off—he was hardly an arsonist if he didn't burn down forests and houses, and he knew that was true because when they caught him for that last fire, they couldn't even call it arson. They couldn't prove he'd started it, they couldn't prove motivation, all they had was a suspect on the scene—and Ronny hadn't disputed that. He hadn't run. He just stood there. As soon as they had him at the station, it became a matter of delinquency; when they cited him, they called it *reckless burning*. That was the term for setting small fires of trash and underbrush: reckless burning. He had a problem with the word *reckless*, but he'd let it slide. That counselor though—he was an asshole for going on about pyromania. What a fucking joke.

Anyway, lately he was too engrossed in the Doctor's experiment to get bored. When the Doctor described the procedure to Ronny, he'd been explicit, repeating the more complicated aspects and defining every scientific or medical term as non-technically as he could. *Wings of grand stature*, he said, *flexible structures fabricated from synthetic skin. PVC skin.* He said *implanted, surgically implanted.* Said, *stitched deep, near the spine, below the deltoids.* There would be a contract, drawn up specifically for the occasion, and it would have to be signed. It would have to be notarized.

Thus the hospital kept him distracted. And Vivian. And of course he'd told her, they'd been in the car less than an hour when he'd told her—it was killing him to keep it to himself. And besides, what Vivian needed to make it through the next eight or ten hours was spectacular distraction. He knew he'd rather have had something like human wings to think about when Pete was gone and he walked the halls of Motherwell High and every asshole he passed made sure to look anywhere, anywhere but at his face.

They were an hour and a half out by then and Vivian was asleep. The night continued, the AM radio voices continued, the dark road continued, passed fields sheened stiff with frost and bordered by the shallow ditches that sloped for miles beneath the moonlit banks. About a quarter mile before they would head southwest, switching over to Highway 5, Ronny veered down the access road to the truck stop. An enormous neon green sign in the shape of a tire, ampersand and spoon was hoisted thirty feet into the sky on a steel pole.

Ronny parked next to a camper and turned off the car. The lot was packed with trucks.

"What time is it?" Vivian said, not opening her eyes. She didn't move, still folded under the coat.

"Not as late as it feels," he said.

"Feels like four in the morning," she said. She squinted her eyes open but stayed where she was.

"Not even 11:30," Ronny said, "Do you mind stopping here, half an hour, is that—"

"Yeah," she said, "It's fine."

They settled at a booth in the corner. The suitcase-brown vinyl of the seats peeled away in slinty patches of cushion shoving through. The table had a series of permanent coffee rings, thirty years' worth of truckers drinking black cup after black cup on their mandatory off-duty. Through the window they could see a bank of rented rooms behind the restaurant. Biblical crosswords were stacked in the revolving magazine rack, along with manuals called *One Year to Savior: 365 Sermons* and gilt-edged Bibles, mini King James versions and large print New Testaments. They sold speed there, too. It was a weird vibe: the low-key desperation mixed with mildly seedy undertones and righteousness.

Edith the waitress brought them coffee and took Ronny's order. Vivian still had no appetite, but when Edith brought Ronny's plate she put a bowl of soup in front of Vivian anyway. Edith had piercing eyes, made more prominent below a wide forehead undecorated by bangs, her blonde hair wisped off her face by a pink plastic clip. Her face was pleasant—her smile an expanse of goldenrod fleshing out a drab meadow—and despite the deep creases under her lower lids, she looked deceptively youthful.

"Now I know you need something, sweetheart, so I brought some soup, you could use it, I can tell."

Edith winked at them and Viv nodded and Ronny thought how she looked like a mess right then, yet her face in sadness was even more lovely than her regular face. Her coalish eyes turned brighter and darker against her pale skin and her normally sharp features were a little puffy from crying.

Vivian stiffly held her spoon, making no move to eat. When Edith came by a few minutes later with the warm-up coffee Vivian drew the spoon to her mouth, swallowed, and caught Edith's eye. Edith smiled, "Good," she said, and left Ronny's coffee steaming at the brim. They sat in silence. Ronny sipped coffee, Viv pushed her soup around with her spoon. Ronny remembered again that he needed to call the Doctor because he wouldn't be showing up the next morning. Vivian gave him a funny look and he paused with his cup mid-distance to the table. And then she was standing up, pushing away from the booth and hurrying to the back, headed toward the ladies' room, the swing door swinging after her.

Ronny didn't know what to do, how long to wait before going after her.

He didn't want to overreact and didn't want to underreact, so he sat there.

Minutes passed and no Vivian. Edith stopped at the table.

"Well she was in such a hurry. Should I go check on her for you, dear?"

She shrugged at the calm room—maybe twelve travelers left but nearly every one tucked into their meals or smoking.

"It's slow," she said. "Just sit tight."

Ronny tapped his lighter on the edge of the table, waiting. He watched a driver on the other side of the room who was playing both sides of a travel chess game. There was something else. There was one thing, one part of it Ronny hadn't told Vivian, back in the car. Not really about the wings, maybe, but somehow related. He had discovered a small safe a few days earlier, when he'd stayed at work late. Ronny had been in the alcove, photocopying an article on dirigibles, when he noticed something jutting out from the wall, a panel that wasn't flush at one corner. He'd pried it open with his keys. What he found inside was a small fireproof box containing old pictures of freak show and sideshow performers, each one (man, woman, child, half-child) awkwardly pivoted under the scaffolding of wings that appeared to sprout from the blades of their shoulders; fliers for exhibitions of rarities, and cabinet cards (circa 1880) of an albino girl named Ida, whose one arm was not an arm but a crumpled, hairless, featherless stretch of muscle that resembled the wing of a skinned chicken. He took one of the fliers. It said LUMINOUS SENSITIVES, COME SEE FIRST HAND. Ronny kept it. Shut the lid, closed the safe, turned out the lights.

Shalt such fever ever last; what lonesome horizon to ignite. Done with twilights that brim with thrushes. Done with cold calls. Done with formalities. Done with potlucks. Done with expenditure reports and standard operating procedures. Done with situation rooms. Done with pundits. Done with hardcore. Done with illustrated guides. Out on the frozen Bodden river, the iceboat skims the clean white scale of erasure: the absence of horizon: the expanse. There is white, and there is white so white it is blue.

Almost like science, how it happened. The chronological reductions, precautions taken against some fierce army's approach. How she started wearing gloves, refusing to touch anything barehanded—newsprint, doorknobs, loose change. Long white gloves that fastened just below the elbow with a single pearled button, hook and eye. She had one pair and every other day washed them in the sink, hands folded on her lap while she waited for them to dry. Or socks pulled over her fingers like mittens. When Vivian asked her mother why she wore the gloves she said, "If you touch something they know where you've been, it's so easy how they can find you. No prints, no trace." She sounded to Vivian like an actor hired to portray a criminal on TV who was still learning her lines. When Vivian asked "Who are they," her mother said, "All of them."

How, a few months before her mother quit that job at the make-up counter of the only department store within city limits, she brought home cans of rice, and beans, and peaches, and bottles of seltzer, and olives, and jars of cashews. She filled the pantry, all the cupboards, the hallway closets and the bedroom closets. She stashed the food under the beds and on the laundry room shelves. For weeks she stockpiled whatever the daily discount was. Soap, artichoke hearts, canisters of wheat germ. Then she quit her job and quit, therefore, leaving the house. She was full of reasons to stay home, to stay inside and prepare for the day they rang the doorbell, the group of them, whoever they were, whatever they wanted—to repo her middle-aged Pontiac? Maybe they weren't even people, maybe what was after her was a darker force.

Once during that season, Vivian came home from junior high—a Thursday, impending snow, the gray afternoon thick with cold, heavy with it—to find that her mother had changed the locks on the door. She tried her key six times, seven times. She rang the doorbell, she knocked, then kicked the door until finally Seth let her in.

Her mother ignored the commotion. Vivian found her in her room, hunched near the window, holding a shortwave radio. The radio was loud, crackling and roaring like wind. Vivian remembered gripping the threshold to keep her balance, feeling like she might pass out.

"What's going on?" she'd said.

"Quick Vivian," her mother whispered, "This is the best place to hear."

Her speech was rushed and declarative. Vivian felt every molecule of her body congregating, rallying against the insanity of her mother crouched there on the floor in sweatpants and blouse and delicate white gloves, staving off whatever doom she was convinced was arriving: Vivian could not move; she stood there staring and suffocating somewhere inside, some place hot and nameless. She couldn't remain, couldn't help, couldn't muster the faith of deciding where to begin. No wonder Seth stopped speaking.

"You changed the locks," Vivian said eventually.

"I know," her mother said, breathless. "I had to, they gave me no choice," she said. "They're almost here."

She touched the window with one gloved hand, like she was waving to someone she knew was out there but couldn't see.

Vivian felt sick remembering, sitting there in the stall, her head in her hands. She wondered how long she'd been in there. She had thrown up in the toilet and instead of feeling better felt light-headed, so she sat down with her head bent to her knees and counted to a hundred twice. When Edith swung through the door, Vivian was staring at the graffiti in her stall. PTL DRIVER CARL SKINNER IS A

"Excuse me, hello?"

It sounded like she sat down on the ledge of the sink, a creaking under new weight sound. PTL DRIVER CARL SKINNER IS A LYING

"You all right in there? Your friend wanted me to check and see are you all right . . . is it your stomach? Do you need anything? There's aspirin at the desk, the truckers always ask for it."

PTL DRIVER CARL SKINNER IS A LYING COCKSUCKER.

Vivian gingerly stood up. Smoothed her tights and straightened her skirt where it bunched up over her knees. She opened the door and went to the other sink.

"It's okay," she said, running the water as cold as it got, holding her wrists under the faucet until she felt calm and sober. The water was too loud to talk over; Edith examined her fingers, chipping pink polish onto the counter nail by nail.

Vivian watched Edith in the mirror. She was not old-looking, but she seemed archaic in that pinafore and nametag, and Vivian would not have been surprised if she had worked that truck stop for thirty-five years by now. And what griefs had rearranged their habits in Edith's life? Was she divorced, was she widowed, did she rent an apartment, eat dinner in front of syndicated *The Love Connections*? Did she put every tip in the jar on her dresser thinking Florida?

"Well," Edith said when the water was off, "You sure got out of there fast sweetheart."

She said "sure" like "shore" and Vivian pictured it that way, a blue wavery expanse rolling open between them, breaking the bathroom sinks apart and drifting them away from each other in big waves.

"What is it, hon, you look like something's spooked you now," Edith said.

Vivian shook her head, more to clear it of the breaking waves she pictured closing in on them.

"I think I just need some water," Viv said.

She thought about saying it, *My mother died yesterday and the last time she talked to me was seven years ago,* but she couldn't bring herself to impose on Edith.

"You're sure now?"

Vivian nodded. She wanted to know if Edith had kids, and if her mother was still alive, and if they talked on the phone.

"Well, I can take care of that. You come along when you're ready, I'll tell your friend."

And she swung out the door, and Vivian leaned on the sink for a minute more because the swinging door was loud and the way it knocked back and forth made her dizzy. She didn't want to think anymore. Two hours down. Eleven more to go. Ronny had lied. It was farther away than Vivian thought.

When they were back on the highway, Ronny tried to think of ways to divert Vivian's attention. She didn't seem to want to talk, but he could tell she wouldn't mind listening. There were other things to tell about Pete, decent things that were not at all tragic. For example, how Pete used to go out in his truck to the back roads which you'd take to get to the river, kind of far out, past the quarry, past the high school maybe thirty miles. He would drive the old truck down to the river—which was mostly a pitiful body of water, not real noteworthy except on the rare days it crested, after rainstorms. Anyway, sometimes Pete would take Ronny with him for whatever reason; he'd take him along. They never talked much, but when they got down there and Pete shut off the engine he'd pull them each a beer from the cooler hidden behind the seat that some kid on the team managed to swipe from his father's garage. Ronny never asked questions. He sipped the cheap beer, which tasted mildly of aluminum and celery, and sat there enjoying the feeling that everything was eventually going to turn out great, the future and everything else. He could kind of see that back then, by the river, in Pete's truck, drinking beer. Maybe three times in all they'd gone down there. Pete went more times than that, of course, usually alone but every once in a while with Mo, his girlfriend. Who knew how his brother decided when to go by himself, when to take someone, when to take Ronny, but Ronny never considered why Pete did any of the things he'd done when he was alive, so he didn't dwell on those kinds of impossible questions since the accident, either. Easier not to, plus you were better off not killing yourself with guesses.

"What about the truck," Vivian asked. "Where is it?"

"My mother drove it to the dump and left it. At the landfill."

"Huh."

"Then she left in the middle of the night two days later. She could've just taken off, herself, you know. I wouldn't mind having that truck around."

And even though he knew why he'd never taken Vivian out to the river, right then, telling her about it, he kind of wished he had. He could picture her down there, just standing there overlooking the busted tires, dead frogs, dying birch trees—at the rim of dirt and brackish water, her wrists pale in the sun.

"He was a good brother, wasn't he?"

She said it so wistfully that Ronny figured she must not have siblings but asked anyway.

"Oh no, I have a brother. Actually—" She paused as if debating how much to say, examining the hole in her tights "—we're twins."

Ronny shook his head. "No way," he said.

She nodded.

"What, then how come you never told me—before? No way," he said.

Vivian bit her lip. She was serious.

"Well, for a lot of reasons," she said, "I don't know where he is. And he doesn't talk."

"What?"

"I mean, yeah, he quit talking. He's mute, electively, so—he no longer . . ."

"That sounds terrible, Vivian."

Viv nodded.

"He's been that way for a long time. You can kind of carry on a conversation with him, because he's good at gestures, but it's hard to not feel bad or weird for him the whole time."

"So he just—" Ronny said, "—one day, stopped talking, that was it, he just gave up—"

Ronny fished a cigarette out of his jacket pocket and used both elbows to steady the wheel as he cupped the cigarette to the car lighter.

She said, "More like, he couldn't bear one more second so he just cut his losses and that's what he came up with. That was his answer. I *get* it, but there's nothing real useful about getting it."

"But when was the last time you saw him or knew where he was?"

She sighed, stretched her sleeves over her fingertips.

"I guess, the night I moved out of my mother's apartment. It was late, I walked out of my room, it was dark except this kind of blue light, which was Seth on the couch watching TV, he used to love to watch

Miami Vice; anyway I walked out and I had a few bags of my stuff and he looked at me kind of surprised, because it was maybe two in the morning, and I'm sure he wondered what I was doing. And there was this second before the door completely shut where I could see inside still, and he had this face like he knew."

She paused for a minute, stared out the window.

"And then I guess later on, I'd mail him a letter to say where I was every time I moved, and for a while, maybe a year or so, I got postcards from him that said how he was, where he was. He was becoming a mime so he traveled a lot and I got postcards from every new show he signed up with, seasonal work, you know. The last place I heard from was Palo Alto. That was, a while ago, at least eight months."

"He's a mime?" Ronny said.

"He's good," Vivian said, "And what else could he do, anyway."

Ronny didn't say anything else, and after a long pause Vivian started talking again.

"I think he got the idea because my mother, her parents worked for a traveling show, so she grew up running games and helping the Alligator Girl out with her booth, selling tickets. She'd tell me stories, how they moved all the time, and the freak shows were the major draw, so her parents—they were show stagers—were always inventing bizarre, fake spectacles. Supposedly they did have one real spectacle, once, a three-legged man. It was so fucked up."

"Wow, Viv. I mean, that's ... pretty nuts."

Ronny could picture it, Viv and the apartment and her mute twin brother and—her mother must have been somewhere in that scenario, too, another voided out sadness, but he didn't want to ask any more questions—the shallow television light and the tunneling silence and the posture of a room no one wanted to stay in, falling shabbier by the hour, lousy with endings, endings guaranteed to collect lousy anniversaries. He knew how those went: the first anniversary of Pete's accident, Ronny skipped school and got wasted in the train yard, of all miserable places. A large fence barricaded the entry but the gate was easy to dodge on foot. Really it was one of the only places worth going, if you thought about it, since it showed you exactly what you wanted to see: burned out train cars, blistered scraps of trash and metal, bad graffiti decorating the pylons, pigeon shit. It surrounded you with ugliness, reminded you how steeped in bland misery the world was; it was pure desolation. He'd sat out there at the east edge of the field where he could watch the flat shunts, and drank his forty, yes, stuffed in a paper bag, and got stoned and was inexplicably—he remembered this clearly—desperately thankful to be exactly where he was that afternoon. The first anniversary of his mother's leaving had been less remarkable, but he'd felt sort of a dull persistence of gloom that whole week, which eventually made sense when he realized how the calendar corresponded. He imagined that was how such occurrences in time evolved: into slight depressions in the ether, or roiling variations in the atmosphere, regions of wind and confusion, horse latitudes of memory that ended up being just vaguely disturbing.

They drove in silence for one hour, two hours, and then the radio pulled the car through the buzz of the desert with its late night dispatches, reverberations of spacecraft machinery, mapped-out sightings of UFOs, and the keening owlish sounds of alien communications. The landscape before them, behind them, surrounding them seemed charged. People called in. A retired NASA engineer described the mechanics of frequency and vibration. A sixty-year-old woman from Nevada reported her cattle vanished into thin air.

"They're all gone, it's nothing left," she said, "None of them, all of it's blackbrush and dust. With my own eyes," she said, "They're gone."

After they'd been on the road for about four hours, as night dwindled to premature morning, there was a forceful thud as the car bucked sideways and the brakes caught hard. Vivian woke up as the car skidded violently off the road into the frozen grass, almost sailing down the shallow embankment separating the road from the forest. The brakes shrieked, pulling the car at a sharp angle: there had been a halting crash, a heavy yielding thump of body striking vehicle, a muscular sliding against metal and tire, unmistakable for what it was. The car stopped moving gradually, stuttering and skidding until tires locked. That was the biggest surprise, how long it took the car to stop. Vivian had banged her knee and shoulder when the car knocked off the pavement. It was still dark, and the highway was empty; Vivian couldn't make out much of what she saw through the window.

Ronny was frozen for a second after the car stopped. When he asked if she was okay, Vivian nodded and answered yes at the same time. Ronny got out of the car, walked back down the edge of the road to the spot where they'd skidded. He bent down to something, knelt like that for a few seconds, then straightened up and headed back to the car. Walked around it looking at all the tires, then flattened his hand on the hood and just stood there. When he got back in the car, he was shaking his head.

"Fucking freezing," he mumbled.

Vivian's voice was a hoarse whisper from having spent the past forty minutes asleep. "What is it, what happened," she said.

"I'm sorry," he said, "We hit a deer. It was small but, she was so fast, I didn't see her, I couldn't really tell what was happening, she just flew out from—"

"Did we kill it?" she asked but didn't want to know.

"I don't see it," Ronny said.

"God," Vivian tucked her feet on the car seat, hugged her knees to her chest, "that's terrible."

They sat there and thought about the poor animal; how it

was probably fledgling and seriously wounded, probably suffering somewhere close by that they just couldn't see or tend to. Now there was an injury between them. They were quiet for a long time. The car wasn't wrecked, but they'd gotten a flat, punctured a rear wheel on a nail or broken bottle. Ronny didn't have a spare. They were stranded until a cop came by or another driver stopped.

Now he'd gone and stranded them, after he'd worked so hard to talk her into this. Here they were just hours in and he'd fucked everything up. Here they were. Inside the car it was getting colder. He looked over at Vivian and even though it was too dark to make out any real details of her face, he could tell she was crying. When was the last time he had fixed anything? He couldn't think of one lousy thing he hadn't ruined, since before Vivian. Before Pete.

Two hundred and thirty miles from the side of the road where Vivian and Ronny waited, the clock flipped from 1:59 to 2:00 a.m. and the Doctor could not sleep. This infuriated him, because he was accustomed to having dominion over his body. Why should he not have unratified power over his circadian sleep cycle, his REM, his melatonin distribution—why must he suffer in this way, he had no patience for insomnia. The Doctor refused to lie there another second, and heaved himself out of bed.

His tugged on his sweatpants, tied and double-knotted his tennis shoes. He would go for a jog—no reason not to exercise the machine that saved the world. No reason not to work the horse the hero rode in on. (The Doctor felt a surge of pride at this one—no idea where he'd picked it up, but he sure appreciated its wisdom.) Yes, people did think of him as a kind of savior, when they came to him desperate to be fixed, or desperate for their son or grandmother to be fixed; that was not an exaggeration. And he must honor their weaknesses, and wield the power of his hands in service of these desperate people.

He was jogging now, down the lane to the end of houses, punching footprints into the snowy grass. His shallow breathing drew needles into his throat, into his lungs. He kept at it, knowing that by a certain kilometer he would succumb to numbness, ease out of this brisk pain.

Many things occurred to him as he struggled down the road—so many things, he imagined he should be grateful to insomnia for earning him these extra hours to ruminate. He was too busy to sleep, *he was working*—those blueprints, for example: he could not decide whether the enhanced dimensions would compensate for the correct amount of lift. Tomorrow they would begin to build the prototype pair, and the failures of design would begin to be made quite evident. He stopped to rest for just a minute; his right leg demanded more stretching. Straightening up, lumbering back off, his thoughts turned to Paul.

Now that they were getting down to mechanics and the fabrication of the ideal, he had to admit he could really use Paul's expertise. The

Doctor admired Paul's commitment to what, as far as he could tell, was a highly specialized branch of ornithology. If he had it right, the particulars of his scholarship were: the morphology of the wings of seabirds (family Hydrobatidae), his specialty within that population being the storm-petrel. Paul was a biologist before he became an ornithologist, and over the past six years he had already completed much work to advance the field; in fact, twice in this short span he had earned the singular award given annually by the oldest professional ornithological association, most recently for a study he'd undertaken in Trinidad and Tobago. Therefore, though the Doctor was acquainted with Paul personally due to the birding classes held at the hospital during the Renaissance Season, which happened every spring—regardless, he would be acquainted with Paul and his work, accolades and all, by virtue of his reputation and the rampant dissemination of gossip in a town this size. Couldn't hide anything around here. And yet—the Doctor smirked at this irony—and yet, a notable man could vanish without a trace in a town this size, too. Not without a *trace*, maybe; trace was not the proper term. The Doctor himself was party to the trace, for one thing—but so far no evidence or suspicion or accusation had turned up nor otherwise been brought to bear by anyone.

The Doctor was walking now, shuffling along and breathing shallow, ragged breaths. Must be three by now, or close to it. He was meant to be headed back home, but he found himself laboring off in the opposite direction still farther, passing the stark blocks of old Victorians, the section of town just north of his own which featured more modest, staid brick colonials. This district was grand and sprawling; the houses spilled over onto themselves, precariously held in at the side yards and alleys. All those turrets and cornices and wreaths.

He found himself on a quiet road and paused to take stock of his exact location, because—there, over that way, down the street where there was a dip that curved off to a stand of trees—that was—no, it was, he was positive, it was Paul's house. How had he gotten this far—again the Doctor felt unnerved by the fact that he'd gotten quite off course. He did not get carried away. Not a day in his life. And yet here he stood, yards from the professor's house. What was this spontaneity he was apparently making a habit of?

He walked closer to Paul's house, keeping to the far side of the street. Dark—of course it was dark. Looming. Of course—it was large by any standard, wide and tall, and right then it looked impenetrable, like a fortress. Not haunted, because that was ridiculous, a westernized co-modification that allowed psychics to turn profits with hotlines. But the deserted house of a missing man, in the middle of the night, everything frozen quiet and amplified in its quietude . . .

"Missing" with quotation marks, the Doctor reminded himself, not *missing*. Not *missing*-missing. Not abducted as the first headlines fretted. Not held hostage, a concern sprung from the edgy local political climate at the time of his disappearance. Not lost, amnesiac and wandering (the hypothesis shared by the Psych residents, and the group of nurse practitioners he often found himself filing into line with at the cafeteria). No. The Doctor knew it was none of these but he remained silent and hardly allowed himself a passing thought about Paul's location and assignment. Barely let the vision of it register: Paul on the most remote island in the South Atlantic, collecting data and serum, consulting the experts in the lab, preparing a compound for the Doctor's wings. Even though his pulse ratcheted higher when he overheard the conjecture at the hospital, he wasn't going to blow their cover. He did what he always did in the cafeteria: kept his eyes off in the general distance; reached for a plastic tray; stepped forward for a scoop of mashed potatoes.

Not like this. Trudging the dark highway, improperly dressed, a few feet from the car. Every step more work than the one before. She left Ronny back there, asleep. She couldn't stand another minute, pretending to be sleeping, pretending to be able to sleep. But she didn't want to die of hypothermia, either. She trudged along the shoulder. Her eyes watered and stung, she could barely see, just kept her head down and barreled into the cold.

She was maybe a tenth of a mile out before she turned back to gauge and realized she could no longer make out Ronny's car in the distance. Her feet were numb and her face felt like it was burning, like it was on fire, and she stopped walking for a minute, needing to rest, because she couldn't think, couldn't move just then, just sank to her knees, needed a few seconds, a minute, of rest. Not sleeping, no, she wasn't asleep—and that large noise rushing over the darkness—fast and large, what was it—a machine like the sky—breaking apart—faster—

She was coming to, and some person was standing there crouching over her, tightening a grip on her ankle, shaking her saying, "Hey, hey listen, hey look at me can you hear me?" Shaking her hard, a person with a hunting cap and a fleece work coat and a thermos on the ground there.

"Hey!" this person shouted.

He was trying to get her up, away from where she was, she was thirsty.

"Let's go," he said, "Over there, the truck's got heat."

He leaned her up, half-carried, half-pushed her, it seemed to take hours but finally she was up in the truck's cab, it was warm, still running, the engine vibrated with steady machine sounds, the vinyl of the seat almost hot. She curled up against it, tucked her knees up to her chin, pressed her cheek flat against the seat cushion and stayed in that position, not moving.

"Hey," said the man, "Are you all right? Miss? You okay?"

He was staring at her. Vivian nodded then stopped and shook her head.

"No, I mean—I don't know what happened."

The truck driver shrugged.

"I don't know either, I saw you fall as I drove by and pulled off, went back to where I'd seen you, this road gets a little deserted overnight.

If you're alone—"

No, not alone, Ronny was back there; she remembered, sort of hazy, that she'd snuck out of the car and left him. She had to go get him, go tell him where she was.

"No," she said, shaking her head carefully, she had the beginning of a headache, "I was back there and I was walking because I couldn't sleep—"

She took a deep breath and started again, "—and we had to wait for help because the car—but . . ."

"So your friend," the man said, "is waiting back there."

He glanced in the big rearview mirror. That's when Vivian noticed she was in a huge twenty-foot hauler, really high above the highway in some truck driver's cab. She hadn't been aware enough to be alarmed and by then it was too late. She figured if he had it in for her, she would already be dead. He was going to let her to live.

"He was asleep," she said.

"We'll see." He pulled the earflaps of his hat over his ears and shoved his hands back into his thick gloves, "I'll walk back and see what's what. Don't move, though."

He started out then leaned back into the cab saying, "Oh here, some coffee in there, better take some—" He poured the cap full and held it over to her.

Vivian leaned back in her seat, her head propped against the window and her legs tucked under. She was so tired, she was so tired. She sipped the lukewarm coffee from the plastic lid. It wasn't good but it was better than nothing.

WHAT THE—WHAT THE FUCK—WAS—

Pounding on the window right next to his head—Ronny jerked awake and registered the fists pounding the glass, over and over before he could register where he even was and what he was doing there—and where was Vivian, Vivian wasn't beside him—he was so confused he didn't roll down the window, he opened the car door and stumbled out, arms raised in front of his face defensively, in case the guy was going to punch him—he wouldn't lay off—

"Man!" he started, "What is—"

The man was telling him to calm down, waving his hand, making a flag of it to stop Ronny shouting.

"She's okay, she's okay, it's fine," the man was saying, "it's fine, it's cool."

Ronny wasn't sure he should believe him. He took a step back, crossed his arms and said, "What is it, then, where's Vivian, tell me what's happening."

The man put his hands up like a shield, interrupting.

"Look, it's fine, but we've got to get back."

"Back—where did you come from?"

Ronny squinted down the road the wrong way. It was brighter already, the morning sunlight glinting off the frosted grass. The man shook his head and pointed out the direction.

"Your car—"

Ronny nodded, kicked at the flat tire. "No spare," he said.

"I bet we can roll it. Might damage the rim, but it's hardly a quarter mile, shouldn't be that rough. Go slow."

Ronny got the car started then straightened out the wheel. It stalled at first but they got it moving. The man leaned on the rear hood and shouted at Ronny to pull out slow; he gripped the underside of the corner and shoved upward, prying the busted tire off its limp frame and heaving it forward to catch pavement.

When it was positioned normal and on the road again, and Ronny got it up to 10 mph, the man vaulted into the passenger seat, and the car stuttered forward, heaving and grabbing at the pavement.

"But Vivian's—"

The man nodded.

"She fell. She's all right. I was headed off the exit, she'd fallen in the snow, just could barely see but I could tell there was this person right there, so I stopped in case there was trouble."

Ronny listened, trying to calculate how much time had passed since he'd been asleep.

"She was almost passed out—she didn't get too far, but the cold, you know—well it's good I saw her when I did. Put her in my truck with the heat."

Ronny nodded, "We're driving to Nebraska. We hit a deer. I did."

The truck driver looked over at Ronny. "There's no . . . trouble here is there? There's no reason she'd be running off like that, then?"

He felt sick as it registered, and shook his head, said, "No sir." Then, to be sure there was no question, he added, "Someone . . . died, we're in a hurry, that's all."

The man nodded. "Up here," he pointed to the shoulder where he'd pulled his truck off.

"I can hitch this up and pull you to the next town, there's a station that could get you the tire. Otherwise . . ." The man shrugged but didn't say anything else.

"Sure," Ronny said. "Then—thanks. My name's Ronny."

"Roosevelt," the truck driver said, sticking out his huge gloved hand, "pleasure."

The Doctor pulled the resin from the top shelf. Almost needed the stool but he got it, nudged the jar to the edge. Spread across all the available counter space, his supplies were like scraps from an alien morgue. A dozen needles in various sizes; makeshift spools of catgut and cotton. A metal tray stacked with thin sheaths of stretched goat hide, pressed and chrome-tanned to preserve rigidity yet remain malleable. A sewing kit. A slab of PVC skin that could be pulped as the subcutaneous layer, depending on the arrangement of wing bones—and for the bones themselves, he would use the rubber and plaster casts he'd made from the delicate leg bones of a doe he'd used as specimens all these decades. A drawer of surgical instruments that looked medieval, even to him: graspers, retractors, lancets, rasps, drill bits, irrigation needles. The Doctor surveyed his materials, paced the room—was there anything he'd forgotten? He'd even remembered the stovetop autoclave.

Directly he set about the task of unfurling the blueprints, which had been furled and unfurled so many thousands of times the paper had softened to transparent in some spots. He'd toted the prints everywhere he went the past few weeks, consulting them too often.

The day had hardly begun, no commotion in the halls, it was too early. Even in such solitude, it was important that the necessary precautions be taken—he knew he couldn't lose sight of the risk. For now the Doctor would shift his arrivals and departures to obscure the hours he'd spend in construction. Not that he was in demand much lately, even during office hours. It seemed like everyone was avoiding him more than usual. No real reason why, far as he could speculate. He'd caused an uproar at the hearing a few weeks back, but that was nothing new—he was perpetually in the minority when it came to radical procedures and ethics clauses and *appropriate dispensation of service and counsel.* Everyone was so predictably short-sighted. He was always on the losing side of an unpopular argument. Even with Lorraine. Lorraine of the sad hands, confiscator of his jogging pants. Which she insisted in sleeping in night after night: so polyestered and unflattering; so elastic-waisted and un-feminine. Elastic-*ankled*, even. Even when he couldn't abide an unfairness some other party was perpetrating, he was the one who lost. And thus, even with Lorraine he had not won. Had merely stepped away from the door as she exited.

One thing he missed about Lorraine: the small of her back where he could rest his hand and feel he was cupping a body ample in its epi-gamic, supple skin. Also: how her neck flushed a butterfly shape down to her breasts, a rash that winged up to her collarbone, after a single glass of Pinot Noir.

But it was better not to reminisce. He paused in his taping—about a third of the goat hide was marked off with masking tape—and decided that what he needed more than anything, right then, right as dawn was breaking, was some very black, very terrible coffee.

The truck was quiet, much quieter than you'd expect from such a large hauler. What were they hauling? He kept forgetting to ask. All three of them crammed across the bench seat and Ronny at one end of it, knee wedged against the door. No one was saying much except for Roosevelt every once in a while starting up with some part of a story involving trucks, highways, diesel stations or Winter Park, Florida, where he had a three-year-old son, Roosevelt Jr., and a girlfriend he might or might not marry, he couldn't say for sure right then.

Vivian stared out their shared window at the road as if entranced as the brisk white landscape spurred by, stark and bright. Ronny didn't want to deal with any extracurricular crises right then. If he could just get the tire fixed, get them back on the road, they'd be fine. They'd move forward unscathed, mostly. But after about thirty minutes in, he shifted his attention back to the other side of the truck and saw Roosevelt's hand on Vivian's knee—just above her knee, then, encroaching at the lisp of her thigh. Way too close. What the hell made Roosevelt think he could get away with that shit? Unbelievable.

He cleared his throat and said, louder than necessary, "How much longer?"

The truck driver looked over at Ronny, calm and measured, half-smirking, as if Ronny was in on whatever the sleazy joke was, and said, "Oh, twenty, twenty-five miles I'd say." His hand didn't move from Vivian's leg.

Roosevelt had turned the tables, and Ronny was fucking pissed. It was fucking harmless and fucking sinister at the same time, and that pretty much covered Ronny's take on things, in general; that was how the camps broke down. Twenty miles to go and now Ronny had to figure out if this guy was a harmless creep or a psychopath, and the whole spirit of the trip—which had been relatively unthreatening, even verging on pleasant—was strained. How much would you rally for a long-hauler, even if he came to the rescue, if he turned out to be a psychopath. Only wasn't that the thing: Roosevelt *was* their good luck. Ronny wanted to punch the guy's face in.

Of course, he wasn't going to punch him, because he felt helpless and idiotic and without much recourse, speeding along the highway locked in the cab. And it was unfair, but he was mad at Vivian for not stopping it, for acting like it was nothing. Christ.

When he looked again Roosevelt had one finger worked up near the hem of her skirt and without letting it even register Ronny said, "What the fuck are you doing? What do you fucking think you are fucking doing?"

And the driver turned to Ronny, still smirking, "Whoa, hold on buddy. Calm down."

"Let us out," Ronny said. "Here, let us out here."

"Listen, buddy—" Roosevelt chuckled and Ronny felt enraged.

"Right here, I'm fucking serious."

And it was surreal because the day was stark white and they were sealed off in the cab, pill-boxed in the sterile middle of it. They were a glacier. They were a glacier still moving—then the trucker roughly pumped the brakes, taking them down over the shoulder where they labored to a thundering stop.

"You're fucking serious, kid? Okay, buddy, get out. Get the fuck out, both you little bitches."

Ronny grabbed Vivian's coat sleeve and pulled her out with him and they sort of stumbled halfway to their knees on the dismal, gelid roadside. The trucker, blasting his horn, roared away with their car.

Ronny gripped Vivian's arm. "What is wrong with you?" he said. And they huddled together, making their way toward the station. Which couldn't be much farther. Which had to be—if the trucker gauged it right—less than five miles off. Screw the car; they'd figure something out. They staggered along. In all the time they'd been on the highway, six cars at the most had passed, all but two of those in the opposite direction.

"Hey," Ronny said.

She kept walking. Ronny still clung to her arm, barely.

"Viv, what's wrong? What?"

He tugged at her wrist, tried to get her to snap out of it. Nothing. He clutched the bulk of her wool sleeve, shaking her arm, but she remained silent, just kept walking away from him, so Ronny drew his breath and shouted her name. He shouted her name, and she continued to walk on though he'd abruptly stopped a few feet back. When he caught up to her, he grabbed her shoulder, obligating her to look at him.

"What do you want?" she said.

The sun was bright, but it was freezing, and he could see that she shivered despite Pete's large coat.

"Why did you let him do that?"

"It doesn't matter," she said.

"Come on, how can you—"

"Ronny. Cut it out. Forget it. Okay? He saved my life, basically, right? It doesn't matter, it didn't matter, forget it. Okay—?" She repeated, "It doesn't matter. Who cares."

She met his eyes, then, finally and her stare was cold and steady and stopped him, lulled an ache up to the bottom of his throat. He cared. Like a fool.

But he nodded and let go, and they kept on walking.

They reached the service station sometime after noon, the sun high, the pavement glistening with pools of ice melt, the snow patches having melted and seeped. And there was the Dasher, rocked up on its better side, a man in a jumper kneeling at one tire.

Vivian hung back at the pay phone as Ronny wandered over to the car, calling out to the man crouched beside it.

The man ducked his head back to catch Ronny's face.

"This yours?"

The man half squatted, sort of in a lunge, to lean on one knee. Wiped his hands on his pants, smearing grease.

"It got dropped off; a hauler left it an hour ago. Said you'd be on your way—left fast as he came, though, nothing else to say to me for sure—"

"How does it look?" Ronny asked. "We hit a deer and blew the tire going off the road."

The man was under the car again; the next time he spoke, he shouted.

"Axle's bent but not too bad, easy enough to fix it. Need a new tire though. Rim's bent too, can't say how rough yet."

"So . . ." Ronny started gauging.

"Take about an hour," the man shouted, "except if I'm less right than I am wrong."

"Right," Ronny sighed.

"Don't worry, Son," said the man, "I'll let you know what we've got soon as I can reckon."

He was still under the car. Ronny couldn't make out his face.

The station had a micro-mart attached to it, a cinderblock building with a few aisles of sundries and instant foods and a half-filled coffee pot on a hot plate. Ronny sat down at the only table, a rectangle propped up against the smeary Plexiglas window on one hobbled leg. The table rocked away from the wall when he leaned with his elbow. He was late for work.

The clock above the register said 1:23 p.m. Five hours late. He wondered if the Doctor had figured he'd chickened out and wasn't coming back. And maybe he'd expected him to quit all along. Through the grimy, fly streaked window he watched Vivian clutch at the phone cord, leaning into the shadow of the booth.

DECEMBER 23, 1989

And how the wind blew. The whole world went white, filled with the sound of the howling wind and the howling wolves staggered along the ridgeline. Every tree icebound and fixed. And there, over there, under the juniper shrub's drooping bough, the hidden entrance to the den. A ribbon of blood shone in the moonlight; a dark apron of shadow obscured one brown boot. One brown boot, the laces shorn wetly, planted a wolf's length away in the snowdrift.

No luck. The operator was helpless, repeating *What city?* and: *I'm sorry, no listings.* Because why would a mute person have a number listed in the phone book, even an elective mute. He wouldn't. Not in California not in Arizona not in Colorado not in Nevada. She could pick any state. It wasn't working. He was nowhere, he was elsewhere, he was gone.

Ronny had walked over from the mini-mart. He waved through the prism of broken glass. A fist had smashed through the window of the booth on the gas pump side and it left a jagged starburst, gum stuck into one dagger, gray and nubbed like an old eraser. She could think of a million things that would make you punch the wall of a phone booth that hard, and felt relieved, mostly, to step away, and make room for Ronny there in that machine built for sobbing and rent, perpetually, with mild trauma. Another outpost. A last resort. Collect calls to hospitals, ex-lovers, cops. Everyone everywhere needed help.

Vivian wandered across the parking lot, kicking at loose bolts and gravel. It was a frigid, restless afternoon. At least now they were stranded with other people, strangers coming and going and every once in a while a kid shouting through the window of a parked car for soda, one parent or the other refueling a Hyundai, eyes on the meter. Not a lot of people, but enough that the world felt lived-in again. Like she and Ronny weren't inherited to some disembodied Midwest, populated by a handful of left-over miseries and a dusty fold of weak-ribbed cows. They weren't staying. They were passing through.

2. The lowest V_3 for each V in the performance area defines a "maximum performance curve." This curve can be predicted by a mathematical model that changes the wingspan, area and profile drag coefficient (CD, pr) of a hypothetical bird to minimize drag. The model can be evaluated for a particular species given (a) a linear function relating wing area to wingspan, and (b) "polar curve" that relates CD, pr and the lift coefficient (C_L) of the wings.

Hypothetical bird. The Doctor underlined that, and after wetting his thumb with the tip of his tongue, he turned the page to read:

Consider a bird gliding at equilibrium at speed V along a flight path inclined at angle θ (the glide angle) to the horizontal (Fig. 1). Only two forces have significant effects on the bird: gravitational force (the bird's weight, W) and aerodynamic force. Since the sum of these two forces is zero, the aerodynamic force on the bird equals the weight in magnitude . . .

His beeper was beeping. Vibrating, actually: across the desk it thumped insistent pauses. SMS: ONE NEW TEXT MESSAGE ARRIVED. He was meant to call a phone number he did not altogether recognize—and who expected him to have time for that, exactly? But, that might be precisely how Paul would contact him—anonymously. Hopeful it was Paul, he closed the report and dialed.

Was it Paul, it would be marvelous timing, for the task at hand was ever increasing in urgency, intensity, scope, and depth, and the day was no longer young; the jowls of the afternoon swung heavily in the manner of a retired bloodhound, unsated, growing restless. At the other end of the line the phone was answered by a young man—not Paul, he knew that at once—no one he recognized at all, and he was about to hang up.

"Doctor, I wasn't sure I could reach you," the voice went, "I'm sorry I'm late, or, I, for not showing up today—"

And he went on, and the Doctor tried to listen, tapping his pencil with his pointer finger impatiently, eager to get on with it. The Doctor was a man who struggled to focus on anything else when he was preoccupied with his premium and macular endeavors. From his office on the fifth floor, he could see clear across to the Dodge dealership. Its large red banner fluttered, announcing a closeout financing opportunity over the parking spaces, little matchboxes of asphalt.

Ronny had been explaining but the wind—was he outside?—muffled enough words that the Doctor had redirected his attention to height equations until a name surfaced over the line, *Vivian*, old-fashioned as *Lorraine*. Lorraine in a garnet dress and her lipstick-rimmed goblet and her pinched-together hands and her insistence on calling a cab that last night, after dinner. He had been too proud to request a parting kiss, and as he recalled her dignified farewell and the shimmer of silk as she pivoted, leaving, he was almost embarrassed. There was a requirement of human dishevelment he could not abide, in himself least of all. He preferred to reside in a world not dictated by romance, but by constants and procedural values.

"Ron," he heard himself interrupting, "nevermind all that. When will you be in? The wingspan data—I begin construction today, and it is dire that the phases are adhered to, the fittings and the trials, Ron, dire, as you are well aware—"

The wind cut him off, though he sat solemn at a desk in a room where no wind circulated.

"Sure," Ronny said, "I know. Friday. Maybe Thursday."

Good Christ, the Doctor thought. It was Monday.

"If you are not in Friday morning, Ron, you won't be needed any day after, so I'm suggesting—that you see to it you return in time."

The Doctor felt upstaged, a feeling that always turned, sooner or later, to extreme dissatisfaction; he grumbled good-bye to Ronny and hung up the phone.

Three days, at the minimum, of solo enterprise. The Doctor was not pleased but would not allow anyone or anything to interrupt his work. After all, nothing as spectacular as wings should be affected by any force shy of catastrophe. The beeper started up again. SMS: ONE NEW TEXT MESSAGE ARRIVED. He was needed in four north. He pushed up from the desk, and reached around the door for his coat.

Four north wing was the wing for malcontents. Not ordinary patients, but those who suffered in a variety of mysterious and arduous ways, most of them ugly. Complicated aberrations piled atop incredible disorders: atrocious cancers that disfigured faces already plagued with tissue over-growth; blind patients who've begun to hear voices and compensate by taking a knife to their skulls and throats (there were two like that); those with corruptive skin and bone ailments that required endless amputation and graft—lip tissue to earlobes, ankle bone to clavicle, eyelids to finger-tips—so that the body came to resemble a puzzle of masterpieces shorn and tethered and retethered. It was not unusual for crudely sculpted misfits to parade the hallway from four north to the foyer of four South (where the dementia patients were housed) in a clumsy progression, harmlessly practicing the stretch and slack of their new skin.

That day, as he rounded the corner of the stairwell and approached the entry, he collided with the door and the man moving dully through it, knocking the Doctor to the side. The man paused there at the second step, turning back to the Doctor, saying, "Doc? Oops. Doc? I'm sorry, Mister—"

And right on the heels of the man rushed a trio of emergency personnel, crowding into the doorway and one of them gripping the man's shoulder saying, "Halt, Vernon. Halt." Vernon was halted already, concerned with the Doctor's injuries, watching him straighten up and wring out his arm which had borne the brunt of the door's force.

The Doctor saw immediately what had been the problem: Vernon headed off four north to find the Doctor of his own accord. In the Doctor's book, Vernon was a magnificent patient. The Doctor had reconstructed his ribcage when it was crushed by a unicorn in the circus—a silver mare forced by the Lakeland Circus Association to sport a nailed-on tusk—when Vernon was catapulted from the cannon thirteen degrees off-target and landed not on the trapeze deck as planned but in the Castle Infinity Pool where the unicorn alternately dashed and strolled.

The mare had lodged her unicorn tusk clear through Vernon's spleen. Vernon's ribcage crumpled, a shoddy wicker basket in the pantry of his torso; the Doctor had to reweave the bones and brace the new cage with a 52-point halter made of steel and held in traction. And Vernon's upper body had mended extraordinarily fast. And Vernon was pleased. But reweaving the bones had required a corridor of jawbone be removed from Vernon's jaw and implanted as sockets where the ribs fused. This caused Vernon a great ache near his mouth, which would not subside. A phantom bone remembered itself to him there, relentlessly. A kind of buzzing sensation but also sometimes the feeling of a feather pressing through his skin, a soft and disturbing transfer like an eternal and mounting restlessness. And, too, a heaviness, which Vernon could only describe as the weight of a suitcase strapped to his chin.

It was an odd, distracting ache, and Vernon grew obsessed with driving it away. The Doctor's remedy: re-cauterizing jawbone and regenerating it, cloning Vernon's bone and resurrecting his jaw from scratch. The hollow would vanish, and all would be well. The Doctor had done a similar procedure with a woman the year before. Mrs. Redspecial. Removed part of her collarbone and replaced it with a coffin bone splinted from a horse. It worked, insofar as it had staved the despair for a missing part. Mrs. Redspecial was pleased. Was declared a success. And given that success, the Doctor believed administering to Vernon with his exact, *replicated* tissue and *replicated* cartilage would present the most fundamental substitution of all. As he'd proposed to the Surgeon's Council that very month: not only did he consider the concurrent operative steps necessary for Vernon's well-being—but treating Vernon was treating a universe of like Vernons with like ailments.

To the interns assembled at the stairs, the Doctor said, "Okay, okay, thank you for the help, the swift action. Now certainly you may relax and return to your duties. We are fine here, everything is fine, fine."

He smoothed the front of his shirt, sweeping his large hand slowly from collar to waist.

When the interns did not move immediately, the Doctor erupted, snapping, "Enough, enough here, go!"

He hated their skepticism, which was rampant, was ingrained in these young know-it-alls. They would want to file a patient report, debrief Vernon, write up an order for restraint. The Doctor reached out to Vernon, tugged his arm sleeved in that immodest, papery shirt, and guided him back to his room.

No collateral. They drove off with empty fists, not even a dollar. A snag in Vivian's tights forged a miniature country over her knee, one more hole. When the car was ready, the mechanic had whistled for them. His sleeves were rolled up, and his arms were blunt tools streaked with dirt and oil. He pressed a stiff paper towel to his forehead twice. Blotted his eyes again, his chin. Ronny waited for him to say how much for labor.

"$172 even," the mechanic announced. "No personal checks."

Vivian handed her money to Ronny, who counted it, added his own twelve dollars, not even twenty, and counted it again.

"We've got—" he unfolded one of the bills, made a smoother pile of them "—$42."

The mechanic shook his head at them. They left the bill unsettled, struck a deal for the balance, an eventual payout plus twenty percent; it was too late to argue. And why not hand over whatever was requested, if you could, was Ronny's viewpoint—now that the price of everything seemed cheap, so long as the wager didn't trade on your sanity, didn't kill or humiliate you, and disguised itself as a choice as much as anything else did, anyway. Choosing a shirt; choosing a lover; choosing to leave. In a way it was all the same, harmless choice after harmless choice: pinstripes; the part-time librarian; after dark.

The mechanic said it would take a good six hours from his station through the Sand Hills north to Valentine. Said it would take six hours but feel like sixteen. Feel like a century. Feel like you took a Klonopin and each minute's as long as four.

"Good luck," he said. "Good thing your car's fixed. Fuel up by Broken Bow. My cousin lives in Merna, and listen, there's nothing out there."

That was true. The sky, splayed so keenly white and threshed to an invisible zenith, deleted every minor thing: the field assembled with its vast epiphany of barren land; a couple trees; a crow; the car with Ronny and Vivian in it. Hard to tell, way out, what was sky and what wasn't, how it settled over the world out there as an uninterrupted sheet of clabbered white. It looked like it would bring snow before the night was through.

At the beginning of the season, the snow would pause for brisk afternoons and resume at nightfall. The earth would clot with frost but thaw quickly to no trace by mid-morning. Eventually winter would kick in and there would be no afternoon respite from the snow and ice, but for now it was basically the bearable part of the cold season there in the plains. Ronny would give it two weeks. After that, forget it. Of course, he'd be home by then. Who knew where Vivian would be.

Flurried movement out of the corner of her eye: a rabbit scurried off to the scrub, a crease of white, Vivian hardly saw it: immediately there, immediately vanished. What poor animals skirted the prairie, furtive and distant, hustling the same spines of dust, dodging trappers, the grand expedition veering ever westward. Ever veering in the name of the next great era, explorers holding fast, wintering their cattle over. Must have homesteaded early, must have salt-cured the hours against unhandsome mouths. The land continued to pioneer a vast and vaster mythology. Burnished of wind and leathered by frost, the hibernating veldt has got its perishables stowed expertly. On and on they drove.

JANUARY 5, 1990

She didn't think about jumping before she did it, the boxcar still moving, the rails of the track rising steep. She fell harder than she'd expected, and faster, rolling down the bank, down to the river still skinned with ice in places, frozen circles like blooms of arctic lichen laced over the dull surface that couldn't hold her. She would slip through the thin ice, sink below, but for now she could still hear the train whistle sounding its mournful warning as she tumbled, jarring elbows and ankles on hard rocks and jagged roots. The last thing she saw was the graffiti in the boxcar lit up from the going-down sun:

get out! Winnipeg 1988.

The mechanic had been right: they did not need directions to get to Valentine. There wasn't much else to get to. When they came to a fork, both roads branched out into rural spokes, more of the same, until signs of civilization crept in. After hours of dust and expanse, there was a laundromat and there was a market. A kid's broken bike in a field. An old chair, heaved up to the road. Every ten miles, a mailbox on a post. They passed a trailer park called Sunset Lakes: twelve or so trailers pulled around a rectangle of gravel and sod; fluttering clothes on laundry lines; a sandbox; a barking dog; a truck. No lakes.

RR 130 was a post office. RR 133 was a barn that had WIG SHOP painted across the front in crooked capital letters. The sun had faded by then and evening was setting in quickly.

"What number we looking for Vivian? 135 . . . that's 137 . . ."

She fished in her bag for that scrap of paper but didn't look at it.

"One-fifty-three." Vivian wanted to be rescued from this—wildly, urgently; now she knew what it felt like to want to disappear, she wanted to just—please—be gone.

Strewn along the gravel road, vestiges of summer castoffs: a kite still snagged in the branches of a palsied tree; a blue above-ground pool hitched between the yards of two modest ranch houses. One looked occupied; the other was boarded up.

Rural Route 144 was a farm, barns stilted way back on acres, pinning down bales of hay and thin cattle. The land grew marshy for a time, then plateaued as they reached a turnoff. Rural Route 153. Ronny almost went past because Vivian didn't stop him but slammed his brakes at the last second and swerved down the drive.

"Okay?" Ronny asked Vivian.

She almost managed to nod but didn't answer.

"Want me to stop here for a minute or something? Just pull off and—"

"No," she shook her head, "It's fine. Keep going."

She didn't know what to say. She felt sick to her stomach. Her heart was beating too fast. She thought she might throw up. She thought her heart might explode.

The narrow road sprawled about the length of a football field, bordered on both sides by a slim gulley. Vivian counted the seconds off until finally, around a bend in the trail, they came to an old single-wide. A weathered awning, dirty white, jutted over the doorstep.

He didn't have to ask if this was the place. He pulled around to the trailer and parked the Dasher and they sat in silence for a long time, as the evening kept on growing darker, and the headlights spilled a vague path through the field, illuminating some odd, scrubby barrelbrush patches that anchored the land. The rest of it faded into the dark: the weak trees, the winding road that lead them there, the trailer itself, its undecorated windows.

It was getting cold in the car. She was having trouble breathing, like she couldn't pull enough air into her lungs—and she didn't know what to do with Ronny, what she'd gotten him into—she couldn't think what to do—but Ronny was looking at her, waiting for her to decide to go in, to stop sitting in the freezing car.

Ronny cut the lights, and they felt their way to the trailer steps, rickety wooden planks stacked up to a platform that functioned as a small porch running the front of the trailer. The awning blocked out the moon as Vivian leaned down and tried the door; for some reason she was surprised that it was unlocked. It swung open, pulling against the vinyl weather stripping with a hushed and sticky sound. They stood in what appeared to be the mini-kitchen—a counter pressed at her elbow from two steps inside the door. She didn't want to go inside.

For the millionth time, Vivian reminded herself that her mother was not there, she wouldn't appear, she wouldn't get angry—she was dead!—but she half-expected a confrontation.

Ronny waited for Vivian to calm down. He touched her arm and said, "It's okay, I'm right here."

Vivian gathered her bearings and reached out, jostling Ronny's shoulder, and felt along the paneled wall, slick and grooved and thinly tacky in certain places, finally landing at the familiar knob of an electrical switch. Muted light fell from a bulb in the ceiling, and as their eyes adjusted, they could make out the squalor. There were stacks and stacks of water-stained boxes and piles of newsprint and junk mail and dirty plates and shoes and encyclopedias and radios—it seemed there was a section crudely cordoned off for electronics, the largest area of the room given over to fractured equipment, antennas, boom boxes, speakers, multi-knobbed hardware, nests of wires, junkyard television sets, miniature satellite-type objects, circuit panels, voltage remotes and walkie-talkies and elaborate-looking headsets. Towers of stuff composed an impasse. A wall. Vivian felt like maybe she wasn't breathing anymore. Every possible surface was covered, every counter, every table, every chair, what the hell. She took a step backward without realizing it and stepped on Ronny's foot.

Ronny reached out to catch her, his fingertips skimming bulk of coat and sweater.

From the far end of the room, a movement caught their attention, a shadow—a person—taking form from behind the boxes, then stepping a large unexaggerated step over a pile of mail and roller skates and decapitated doll heads, and moving forward, through the sea of junk. Vivian was frozen in place, waiting for the glint off the knife he would brandish, surely, braced to make a run for it—

And there in the middle of the trailer stood a thin man in an oyster-colored button-down, the tail end of it hanging past jeans that dragged over faded Hi-Tops. His hair hung to his chin, sharp and straight, blond like rough straw; he shook it away from where it fell over his eye, and waved a shy wave, one hand at his heart like pledging allegiance.

Every.   So   Several.
Every   Every   Hello
To   Arrive,   Surprise,
Now.   To   Arrive,
Sudden,   How   After
Long.   Lost   After
Several,   After   Every,
After   How.   Vivian
Don't.   Don't   Cry
Don't.   Viv.   What
Vivian.   Stay   Vivian.
It's   Me   Don't
Viv   Don't   Cry
Vivian,   Don't.

It was Seth. Of course. She should have known—of all the places she thought Seth might be, she hadn't considered that he'd ended up here, but of course he would have; of course she would be the last to know, the last to arrive. Vivian wiped at her face with her sleeve and when she could she said, "Ronny this is Seth. Seth this is my friend Ronny."

Ronny could not have prepared himself for how striking the resemblance would be, despite Seth's blond hair. He shook Seth's hand; it was a normal handshake, not an acted-out mime-type handshake. Ronny was relieved. But after that he just stood there, hands in his pockets, and Seth stood there, shifting his weight, and Vivian stood there wiping at her face with her sleeve.

Behind a screen of stacked boxes was a couch, orange and tan and overstuffed, somehow crammed at the back of the room, which is where Seth had been taking a nap, apparently. She and Ronny sat at one end and Seth cleared a space on the floor, dislodging a box of batteries, metal levers, parts of old telephone receivers, and the cast of a prosthetic arm. Vivian and Seth passed a notebook back and forth. Vivian asked questions and Seth wrote his answers in shorthand.

"When did you get here, how long have you been here?"

Suddenly, Two Days Ago.

"Where were you before two days ago, I called and called and got nowhere with the operator?"

Las Vegas Most Of The Time

"Las Vegas?"

Las Vegas. Mostly Vegas.

"How did you—? How did you hear—the news?"

No. No News First, Several After Several.

"What? No news first? What does that mean?"

Not First, Then This. Suddenly. Sure Any Problem. No Problem.

"Have you eaten? Is there food?"

Yes Food From The Neighbors.

"The neighbors who found the goat? Who found her—here—and?"

Yes.

"The neighbors who found the goat brought you food?"

Yes.

"Where is the bird?"

Seth shrugged.

Vivian closed the notebook; they weren't really getting anywhere. She punched Seth harder than she meant to on the arm.

"I can't believe you're here," she said. "I'm so glad you're here. I didn't know, I had no idea how to find you, and just, it's been so long."

In a minute she said, "Las Vegas, really?"

Seth pantomimed slot machines.

"Shit," she said, and laughed, "Of course."

It felt strange to be in her mother's place, without their mother, and Seth—it made sense that he had gotten there first; their mother had always liked him more. And who cared, now, anyway, she was just glad he was there. Soon Ronny would leave and she dreaded being there alone.

Ronny—she wondered what he was thinking about, what she'd gotten him into, now that he was here in the middle of it. There they were, on the weird couch, hemmed in among the wreckage, the ton of it, gleaned from charity shoppe rubbish bins or lifted from dumpsters or ditches, who knew, but the mountains piled up around them, ugly and precarious.

Almost an hour of hauling and rearranging allowed a space for sleep. Minus phonebooks, transistor radios, extension cords, and pre-Soviet Union globes, the carpet appeared in scraps the color of clay. Carpet that was gritty with birdseed. Picnic's empty cage propped up on a box the size of a mini-fridge in the room that would have been the bedroom had there been a bed or mattress; there was neither.

They turned in early, exhausted from the drive and the wreck and the arrival and the reunion; they took Ronny's sleeping bag from the backseat and used Pete's coat as a blanket. Seth took the couch in the main room.

In the dark, lying there, Ronny and Vivian were quiet for a long time, not sleeping. He wondered what he could say. She stared at the ceiling. Propping himself up on one elbow, leaning over to Vivian, he brushed the hair out of her face, and she reached up to catch his arm and held it, her fingers lightly clutching his wrist.

"Are you all right?" he said.

She pulled his wrist to her mouth, to her lips, and held on to him like that for a long time.

"I don't know," she said eventually, giving his arm back, rolling over, folded back into shadow, away from him.

They had come to an ending, her and Seth and even, kind of, her and Ronny. She'd never come to an ending before. That night was a broken machine, hour after hour of no good reason, no reason, what if there was nothing left to save.

Ronny hadn't slept great, and he wasn't sure what he was doing there now that a whole new day had started. So much of the plan had been getting there, but then what. If he drove straight through, it would take him a whole day to make it back. If he left first thing the next morning, he'd get to work by Friday, 8:00 a.m. Get back to the flight trial, get back to actually testing out the prototype wings, leaving Vivian to deal with what, in the daylight, was excruciating. Claustrophobic. He had to keep stepping outside onto the feeble porch every few minutes, and they'd only been at the dishes an hour.

A minibar of hotel soap was all they found that could count as cleaning supplies. Vivian soaped and Ronny rinsed.

What Seth did or merely demonstrated: Like smoking. Like archery. Like Qi Gong exercises. Like carrying a cumbersome box down a spiral staircase. Like dealing a hand. Like discovering Picnic the bird under the front steps. Like taking inventory. He unstacked and unsealed, and box by box examined and labeled the contents of each: DOLL PARTS, HAMMERS, FLASHLIGHTS, RABBIT FEET AND HORSE SHOES, CUTLERY, POCKET KNIVES. Seth got through nine cartons and barely made a dent—there must have been close to thirty left. He almost let himself hope to find something that had been his: a soccer ball, a Megadeth T-shirt, some souvenir from his life pre-mime.

He was okay, Ronny decided; Seth was okay. Not as bad off as Ronny'd expected. He'd pictured him in a costume, tights and turtleneck, soft, noiseless shoes—not as a normal guy who happened to be extra silent. When you saw him from farther off—like when Ronny went outside to smoke and wandered down the yard awhile, and looking back there were Vivian and Seth, sitting on the front porch—it just looked how regular conversation looks from a distance. Vivian's jean jacket was a little short in the arms. As she talked, she gestured and her wrists jutted out from the sleeves, anemic birds. Seth leaned against the trailer listening, his arms still for once, not illustrating anything. From where Ronny stood, there might not be any tragedy at all, and there might not be any mistakes, and there might not be any grief.

Nine hundred and sixty-two letters, canceled and returned. They counted them. Addressed to Compound, to Headquarters, to Treasury: Quest for AI, Corona, New Mexico. Vivian read twelve, barely legible in faded pencil cursive—pleas for information about unknown life forces; pleas for support of an unnamed mission; pleas for technical assistance regarding the harnessing of shortwaves. *August 1983 Quest for AI Headquarters Dear Whom it May Concern, Near the feedlot down Sedgewick the rattling, at dawn, was loudest, like chimes, an ugly high-pitched sound no echo—and stars collapsing, They engineered an Astronomical Arrangement, They are starting The Experiment I have evidence . . . January 1985 Quest for AI Headquarters Dear Whom it May Concern, then lights all in halo, they are preparing the last nation of destiny I saw the wavy lines the glowing wavy radiation yes the land is radiated all the way to the bridge by Darby's store at a degree of 45 watts Trillion. This hyper-radiation . . .*

Vivian skimmed them, looking for anything useful, but it was all the same. *Dear Whom it Concerns, The soil has been replaced by synthetic poison soil, delivered to cripple the town's good people who harvest in danger . . . the forces an alarm and I implore you to launch a full investigation . . .* Twelve rambling missives, twelve identical Sincerelies and no name given, just initials: A.K.

"That doesn't make sense," said Vivian, "Her initials aren't A.K. Her initials are E.F." She said it to no one; Ronny was on the porch smoking and Seth was out in the woods somewhere, who knows. Nine hundred and fifty letters remained and chances were they were all just more of the same. What could she hope to learn from that kind of desperation? It was depressing and useless. It was unnerving, the scope of the illness, how it had left so many busted radios and suspicions in its wake.

Late that night, Ronny and Vivian waited in the dark, not sleeping. They were waiting for something to happen is how it seemed to Ronny, not talking, not sleeping, not making out, their last night together, for who knew how long. They waited. In the claustrophobic dark of their makeshift room, the inanimate army hulking in the pitch, hardly kept at bay. In every direction there was a taxidermied rabbit to trip over or a stack of VCRs to knock down. At night, you couldn't see it anymore, but it got worse because you felt it encroaching.

"What are you going to do?" Ronny asked Vivian.

"What do you mean?" Vivian said, "Do what."

She sounded distracted, defensive. He could tell she was hardly even in the room. Of course she wanted to disappear. He didn't say anything else.

"I need a favor," she said suddenly, "can you check on Helen's house and mail and everything, the plants, until I get back, a week maybe, you can take the key? Just in case there's news, from her husband, or anything . . ." She trailed off.

"Sure," Ronny said.

And right then he thought of Christmas for some reason, even though it was still weeks away. What would the holidays look like out here in the middle of nowhere, a sad junkyard of a celebration, an X'd out culvert, no one bringing over casseroles or whatever. It would be more depressing than the holidays he shared with his father, even, and those were almost unbearable. His father would pull out the stockings they'd had as kids, him and Pete, hang them over the fireplace, the ones with their names sewn on, and no matter how Ronny looked at it, nostalgic or not, that was fucked up. That was the weight of magnificent debilitation; that was a man being killed by grief.

FEBRUARY 12, 1990

According to the fulminologist, there is a region in northern Brazil known as the Flash Lightning Flatlands. Chapadu do Corsico. In the US, the ribbon of Interstate 4 between Orlando and St. Petersburg is known as Lightning Alley. The fulminologist held a *National Geographic* up to the class of fourth graders, opened to a spread of forest. *See that*, he pointed at the gaping scar leeched into a massive tree trunk. He snapped his fingers. *Have you ever heard of a Lichtenberg Figure?* He drew the word out for them, lick-ten-burg, of course they'd never heard of one. He took a photograph from his briefcase, moving close so each child in the class could see the spot on the tree where his finger pointed. Scalded into the bark, just three letters. VMF.

When Vivian woke the next morning Ronny wasn't asleep next to her.
She found him on the porch, smoking and trying to follow something
Seth was saying (not saying) about the car. Ronny had no idea what he
meant, so he nodded and shrugged at the same time.

"He wants to know about your mileage," Vivian said, leaning onto
the front steps from the doorway, surprised by how relieved she felt to
see him there, afraid he'd left already.

"Oh," Ronny said, "not great. Something like seventeen to the
gallon."

He took a long drag on the cigarette, looked back at Vivian.

"Hey, don't think I would have left without telling you—"

Vivian's arms were folded to her chest. Of course he'd planned
to take off.

"Just, I need to get going, you know." He ducked his head. Studied
something about his shoe, or the porch. She sat down next to him, scraping her ankle on the rotting wood. The skin pearled red instantly, gave
her something to concentrate on.

"Do you have a phone here? That works? A number?" He didn't
know why he hadn't checked before. Probably because he hadn't needed
to call anyone; he'd bet on his life his father hadn't noticed he'd ever
left town.

She nodded, watched Seth way out near the gulch lobbing rocks at
a tree. He struck some imaginary target between the two lowest branches
over and over with impressive precision. You could hear it.

"I'll call you if you want," he said after a little while. Vivian nodded.
She kept staring out at the edge of the woods.

Ronny walked to his car, got a marker, walked back. He wrote her
number on the back of his hand and said, "I'll call you." Like he had to
convince somebody. Vivian was trying to remain stoic, not looking at
Ronny, because the prospect of being left alone right then . . . because
then what? Then what.

She counted the snaps of the rocks as they hit the tree and split
bark. At eleven Ronny stood up, put his hand on Vivian's shoulder.
Didn't say anything, just stood there for what seemed like a long time,
then bent down to kiss the top of her head. She tilted her head back

and he cupped her chin, leaning to her mouth, the smoky warmth of his breath, she tried to memorize the space they held together where they touched, that pulled at them, because too soon he was letting go, gently, moving away, backing slowly down the steps. He waved from the car, just once, pulling out. Vivian felt a molecular yearning, like something wrenching wide open inside her stomach and the backs of her knees. At the turnout, he paused and exchanged high-fives with Seth, reaching his hand through the open window.

Whatever light was left in the sky was turning to wax. Pinpricks of virga constellated the windshield. Thin frost sheening the car, the flatlands. But the pavement was too warm for the ice to take. And he'd driven all the way to the edge of the state, made good time, hardly stopped—four more hours and he'd be more than halfway back. Seventeen cigarettes, some crackers, a Mountain Dew. One dilapidated rest stop where the overhead bulb was curtained with webs and the sinks had obviously been used as urinals for years; vending machine chips; the drone of static on every station. Just as dawn was breaking, Ronny pulled into town. It was like he'd been gone for months, how monolithic every familiar landmark was, rising through the fog: the bus depot, the gate to the quarry road, the high school, the law office, the movie theatre, the pawnshop, the YMCA. He drove slowly down his street, careful not to glance in the direction of Helen's empty house. He had meant to call Vivian from a pay phone, once he'd gotten far enough away that he was definitely gone, but then he'd just kept driving. Because the thought of her voice, stuck in that trailer kitchenette—how exhausted or resigned she might sound, how despondent—he would have gone back for her. So he kept driving. Which felt terrible, having arrived.

He cut the lights as he swung into the driveway, from habit, from when he used to sneak in after curfew that last summer of high school. House looked the same, yard looked the same—a relief he hadn't known he'd hoped for until there it was, all of it the same, and he felt his shoulders slacken. He passed his father's office on the way down the hall: not a sound. Back in his room, he'd barely stretched out on the bed before he fell asleep in his clothes and shoes and slept for a very long time.

The record crackled and spit as the needle traced over its grooves, falling in. Ronny sat on the floor of Pete's room, leaned against the bed, record sleeve beside him. The Rolling Stones. Even the very beginning of the song that was playing made something inside him feel like it was coming loose. His spleen, his kidney. All that unbearable distance, all that business about being withheld. Sure—maybe arrival and reunion were inevitable, eventually, but in the meantime you were dying. And you could hardly stand it. You collapsed, keeled over. You gave up.

Looking around the room Ronny had the feeling of being pressed upon by some heavy thing. He'd slept all day and woke late afternoon, disoriented, sweating. He hadn't been in Pete's room in months. His father never went in, as far as he could tell. He'd left it intact and shut the door. Records and books were stacked where Pete left them. Like he took off yesterday. Helmet on the desk; a jersey draping the back of the chair; papers, notebooks, normal desk type things—it all took on a surreal, acute presence; it was like a reenactment. Nobody would use the stapler again, the lamp, the dumb remainders. All of Pete's things demonstrated the idea of former action. On the bookshelf: Pete's model airplane collection, fighters in formation.

That song ended and another began, the record turning simple revolutions, multiplying them. At the end there was a choir and all the swelling voices made Ronny think of those buckets you kept clams in before shelling—tall, putty-colored buckets—made him picture those buckets full of human hearts being spread over the deserted winter beach. The hearts kept beating, still pumping blood, pushing fist-shaped divots into the sand.

The room grew dark. He put on Pete's helmet, sat back down. The voices of the choir rose, loud, and Ronny felt the buzz of the speakers heating up, of the afternoon cracking, of all those hearts being raked out to sea. Without meaning to he'd been thinking of Vivian, wondering if she was going to ever make it back, if she'd talk to him if he called, and what would her voice on the phone make him feel like—his head ached, he was dehydrated—the music was so loud it seemed to pulsate inside him, shift inside his blood. He hadn't heard his father at the door, but suddenly he was standing there. He just stood there. Ronny panicked and didn't move. His father leaned against the doorframe, then slid like a loaded sack to the floor where he kneeled, slumped over.

"Dad?" Ronny said quietly, alarmed.

Tucked into himself like that, his father sort of rocked back and forth. Ronny sat there. After some time, his father lifted his head and his eyes caught on Pete's helmet. He reached over, rested his hand on the side of it. Ronny handed it over and his father clutched it to his face like it was a mask. Ronny could only make out one of his father's eyes when he did that. The music continued to pour into the room.

Ronny couldn't hear what his father said a little while later when he finally spoke; the music was too loud, or the helmet muffled his voice, but Ronny knew what he was saying. Knew from the lines around his eyes and mouth that drew tight then gaped loose, ugly with the words as he pronounced them. The helmet dropped to the floor, cracked loudly on the hardwood. For a long second Ronny could see through the man, could see the face beneath the skin, the bones that held his shape, his skeleton, his skull, the ghost beneath his body. The ghost he would become. *Where did he go* the voice was saying, not asking, it was just moving to form those words *where did he go* over and over and Ronny stood up, put a hand on his father's shoulder, then both hands, what was he supposed to do. His father's body shook. Ronny closed his eyes, shut the words out, and pictured the room going up in flames, the house in flames, the yard, the street, the neighborhood, the high school, the whole town burning.

When he had first conceived of them, the Doctor envisioned the broad slate-tipped wings of a crane, as if all that needed doing was to transplant and affix the actual wings of an actual crane—sweeping, enormous appendages—onto a human being. As if the transplant *in and of itself* was an industrious achievement. The contraption before him bore little resemblance to the wings of any avian creature—they were more pterodactyl, these honeycombed, fleshy sails. He'd woven the sheaths of goatskin into two isosceles triangles, then sewn them with catgut to bind the fibers. The edges that would become the shoulder blade extensions were reinforced with a paste made from resin and polyurethane and the shoulder blades were filed, then buffed, then filed, until they reached the perfect thickness and gauge. To attach them required that the skin of the back be split into flaps, stretched with a retractor and re-shaped using the deer leg brace (either sewn or bolted), which would be grafted vertically along the spine.

Of which the Doctor was proudest: the long base edge of the wing. Scalloped, shallow ridges remained unstitched to enable contour and drift. A series of oblong air pockets could inflate to establish lift and stabilize float. The Doctor was ecstatic with his design and his craftsmanship, and restless with anticipation for the flight. He didn't even mind that he would spend that night on call, as he knew for certain he'd be incapable of sleep regardless.

What would ensue that afternoon: a contentious board meeting; a Code Silver on the ninth floor (false alarm, truncated evacuation: by the time the Doctor reached the second flight of stairs it was already time to turn back); rounds; three and a half cups of vending machine coffee; a tepid meatloaf for dinner in the cafeteria, spent at the head of a table crowded with PTs.

Therefore, come dawn, the Doctor strode wearily across the parking lot—it was freezing outside, the temperature had plummeted ten degrees overnight—and approached his Nissan Maxima where he'd left it two days prior. About to toss his briefcase into the backseat, he stopped, one hand on the door. There was a person in the passenger seat. He could just make out the figure's profile, his shoulders, one arm extended—

He scrambled, grabbing at the door faster than he could actually move, his clumsy, sleep-deprived body getting in the way—he couldn't believe it, he couldn't—

It was Paul, heavily-bearded, looking sheepish, tired, in need of a meal. The Doctor jumped into the driver's seat and slapped Paul on the shoulder.

Paul managed a polite chuckle before his face stiffened and he grimaced.

"Did you spend the night in the car? What's that? You all right there?"

"Oh, my ribs," Paul fake groaned, "it's from the airlift, when I was getting pulled out and dropped at the port, you can't believe how those guys hustle—it was intense Doc—anyway, they dropped and the cables—"

The Doctor nodded, "I can tape that up, should be all you require. For your sake let's hope you've just got a massive bruise instead of broken ribs. You're back just in time!"

He fumbled to start the car, too enthusiastic.

"Wait," Paul reached over, placed his hand on the Doctor's arm to get his full attention. "You've got to see this."

He shrugged out of the coat he was wearing and leaned back so he could reach a small cork-stoppered vial from the pocket of his chinos.

"This." Paul opened it, tapped a pinch of gray powder into the Doctor's palm.

"Go like this."

The Doctor rubbed his hands together, turning the powder to a thin gummy paste that coated his skin.

"Tree paste. Endemic to the volcanic islands, weather-resistant, organic, pliable. No interference with aerodynamics . . ."

The Doctor slammed his fist on the dashboard, ecstatic.

"This is *it*. And my god! A feat in time."

"Well, it took longer than expected, but that should be the best waterproofing for any material you use. And it's too viscous to affect glide."

"And not a minute too soon," the Doctor said. "Paul, I daresay I am damn near giddy."

Once at the Doctor's house, after the Doctor had taped up Paul's ribs, they retired to the living room where Paul fought to stay awake, prostrate on the couch. The Doctor paced the room and interrogated his new guest on the past three and a half months he'd been hiding out on the island, working on the compound. Had he compromised his plan at all, or come close? Had he found himself in danger at any time? Had he made any attempts to send word to his wife?

"I've had no contact with Helen. Come on, I've taken every hour of this experiment more seriously than my marriage for months. Seriously, forget it."

Paul's eyes were closed; one arm rested across his forehead, shielding his face.

The Doctor sighed and reluctantly left Paul to sleep. He relocated to his study where he continued to pace.

It was still dark the next morning when Ronny headed out to the hospital. He didn't want to see his father nor delay his return to the lab another minute. When Ronny reached the fourth floor he slowed his pace, put off, as always, by the antiseptic odor and the harsh lights. Mint green walls the color of sickness; of fevers, respirators, hospital food and the trays that served it. And too many anatomical melancholies. Every possible failure of the body and spirit infiltrated these beds and corridors and syringes.

It was only slightly a relief to pull the lab door closed behind him. At first Ronny was confused. The lab was empty and everything looked exactly the same. He wandered back into the alcove, back near the supply closet where he'd found the safe, and was deciding whether to check it out again when the door opened and a man walked in. He was clean-shaven and deeply tan, oddly complected for that Midwestern winter morning. Who the hell was he, and what did he think he was doing? Ronny nodded at the guy, folded his arms across his chest, and the guy didn't say anything, and they kind of stayed like that, in a standoff, until the Doctor burst into the room a few minutes later.

"Oh and so then you have met already," the Doctor said.

"Actually we—" Ronny started.

The Doctor was ebullient, striding across the room to clasp both men by the shoulders.

"Ronny, you are returned last minute—and none too soon, I must add—but let's put that behind us now; and also here's Paul, who now you understand is something of a mastermind and partly responsible for our invention."

Ronny couldn't believe it: *This* was the missing husband? But shouldn't someone contact the police—shouldn't he call Vivian who should call Helen—

"Listen, listen to what Paul has done to enable our current experiment," the Doctor said.

"He's traveled, in great secrecy, his disappearance manufactured, to Tristan Da Cunha. From this island he's recovered material that will weatherproof the wings almost weightlessly, to retain aerodynamics and durability in extremely variable weather conditions, at any height—this is the magic *bullet*, Ron, if you will."

Paul shrugged, like he was acting humble and nonchalant about this praise, but Ronny bet he considered his role quite remarkable—he already knew Paul was an asshole because unless Helen was in on it, Paul had faked his own disappearance and escaped to some obscure, apparently tropical outpost in the name of the Doctor's experiment—which was definitely some kind of fraud, and besides that, it was lame. And the other thing was, Paul's resurfacing displaced Ronny. He'd been integral before Paul showed up. Before Paul showed up heroically. In time for the major unveiling of an extraordinary, spectacular, never-done-before thing.

The Doctor was in such high spirits he slapped Ronny on the back, which Ronny guessed he meant to be friendly, and made to grab Paul's shoulder before stopping short to utter something about the state of Paul's ribcage. Ronny was tired of the show, ready to get on with it. He cleared his throat to get their attention, but when the Doctor and Paul kept on about the Tristan Albatrosses, he gave up, ducking out of the lab and heading downstairs to smoke.

When he got outside, he could tell something was different; the mood was off. Usually it was the same group of housekeeping staff and nursing aides out there by the benches, on break. Ronny generally recognized a few of them, once or twice having bummed a cigarette. But that morning, besides the woman from the gift shop, it was a new crowd. A crowd that looked like doctors and residents and interns in scrubs, pagers holstered to waistbands. A few smoked; most sipped from diet soda cans or Styrofoam cups. It seemed like a meeting, but meetings were usually held formally, behind closed doors, not out on a smoke break where anyone could wander within earshot. As Ronny had, standing off to the side and apparently unnoticed by the group, they were so engrossed in their gossip. Right away Ronny could tell it was worse than he'd thought.

One guy said, "No, I don't know if it's a matter of endangerment or more of a misdemeanor maybe—"

And a tall guy with an earring interrupted, "I bet it's nonsense, come on, what revolutionary good could possibly come from that—"

Someone else chimed in, "Nutcase?"

And there was a subdued wave of amused agreement. Someone clapped.

Ronny tried to make sense of what he was hearing.

". . . full of methods that aren't supervised. It's against policy, not to mention against . . ."

"If we could get photographs, or records, document whatever—"

"Hey, Adam, what we need is to drag Mead in on this—" he paused to check his beeper "—he'd have the legal part nailed in less time than we'll need to get—"

The reasoning continued. Ronny hoped he could get out of there as invisibly as he'd joined. He was pretty sure he knew who was causing such uproar and conspiracy theorizing among these hospital workers. Who else? He concentrated on smoking. Fought an urge to drop the cigarette to the dead leaves at his feet, though his hand definitely itched. When he'd finished his cigarette, he took a few casual steps, quietly opening up a safe distance between himself and the group before muttering how it was much later than he'd thought, and jogging the rest of the way to the door.

MARCH 18, 1990

She was in the basement of the library's main branch when the earth-quake struck, browsing in the Mourning Archives and researching min-iature eye portraits. THOUGH LOST TO SIGHT, TO MEMORY EVER DEAR. The Prince of Wales prepared a token of his love for the widow he was forbid-den to marry. Through the spring, the summer, the fall, the winter of 1785, he wore his lover's portrait eye in a locket under his lapel. There was reason to remain anonymous. Among the books scattered next to her, around her, on top of her were the following: *Tokens of Affection and Regard: Daguerreotype in American History Photography*; *The Victorian Postcard*; *Collector's Encyclopedia of Hairwork Jewelry*; and *Mourning Dress, A Costume and Social History*.

The voice on the other end of the line had sounded stern though not unkind. It was a two and a half mile to walk to Richard Santiago's Funeral Home, where some person (presumably Richard Santiago) would reach into the cabinet (or sideboard, or console) to present her with a cylindrical container resembling a coffee can. Which she would have to accept, then carry two and a half miles back, an exercise in forgiveness she dreaded.

No cars passed, no trucks on the road as she scuffed along. The land in the distance was stacked in striated browns, tans, coppers, darkest where the banner of sky met the dirt horizon. A mile in, she turned at the post office, the only significant landmark from her mother's end of town. The deserted end; Richard Santiago had called it that. Nothing for a long stretch, then the post office, then a service station/Italian deli/video rental place, the type of three-part venture you find at the beach.

Eventually she came to the strip mall where Richard Santiago's Funeral Home was wedged between empty storefront and vacuum repair shop. She rang the bell and was buzzed inside and found herself dwarfed by the cavernous room. Vivian waited, walking a slow circle around the perimeter. It was vast as a ballroom and high-ceilinged; folding chairs stacked against the back wall; the floor scuffed from years of high heels and chair legs. It felt like a warehouse for storing funereal accessories, not like a place where funerals might occur—it was too Rec Hall. She noticed a door at the back. Maybe that was the storage room for the uncollected ashes, shelves lined with boxes labeled with names of the forgotten deceased. (Because what happened to a person who died alone in the world? What etiquette for the loners and misanthropes; were services held for empty rooms? Her mother was exactly the type of person upon which a grievers-for-hire industry might be built.)

Richard Santiago startled her and she spun to face him, a short flask-shaped man in an oversized suit, who caught her fingers in a weak clutch, saying, "Let me offer my condolences to you, Miss; loss is a darkness to excavate, but the gift of grief is, yes, a gift that does eventually bestow much light, I dare say, and your gladdening faith ensures your dearly departed's eternal peace."

Richard Santiago bowed his head to indicate the conclusion of his speech. Vivian didn't think that was quite how it all worked but managed a nod which seemed equally respectful and noncommittal. She nervously smoothed her hair behind her ear. *Richard Santiago* was inscribed on a plastic nametag pinned to Richard Santiago's lapel. He gestured the way and Vivian followed slowly to the funeral home's back office. Where Richard Santiago flipped a light switch; rolled out a chair on wheels; handed her a clipboard and a ballpoint pen.

The form was based on the technicalities of death: her mother's name and date of birth and social security number (left blank; Vivian did not know). Certain facts already auto-formatted (time/date/cause of death) transferred from the caseworker's file. An endless signature line coupled with a place to print VIVIAN MERRITT FOSTER. The fee was $135, and the urn Richard Santiago tried to sell her was an unwieldy $78 sculpture, purple ceramic flanked by doves in bas-relief. Mrs. Randall had generously donated $20 when she'd dropped off groceries, but that left Vivian $15 short for her mother's ashes. Her mother's ashes: the most embarrassing thing to be a few dollars short for in the history of currency or economics or grief.

Richard Santiago unpinched the clipboard and slid the form into a file and excused himself to the back of the room, which was lined with shelves of recycled cardboard cartons. Richard Santiago plucked one from a mid-level and walked it back to her. She had nothing to barter, nothing to trade, not enough to pay with, but this was her gloomy heritage; she couldn't forfeit.

Richard Santiago was writing out a receipt on an old-fashioned carbon copy machine, preoccupied with setting the ledger straight. He'd already handed Vivian the certificate of death in a manila envelope, which she tucked under her arm, and she already clutched the box tagged *33022GN_Evangeline Foster* in her hands. Fuck. She was going to do it.

She counted to ten . . . fifteen . . . twenty . . . twenty-five . . . backing up to the office door, the open door, she turned . . . twenty-six . . . twenty-seven—and took off. She ran through the building, outside, all the way across the parking lot of the mini-strip mall, which had turned out to be of the dollar store/bakery outlet/discount medical supplies variety. She couldn't hear if Richard Santiago tried to stop her; her brain was full of blank rushing, a loud and buzzy nothingness. She caught her reflection in the display window of the Rehab-Mart—cluster of walkers, bedpans, blood pressure test kits—as she raced by, as she tried to pretend she hadn't just stolen her mother's ashes.

Good grief, the nonsense! The boy was full of misapprehension. What had gotten after him? One smoking break—was he defecting, was that what this was about? The Doctor sighed, on the verge of losing his patience. Paranoia was not atypical for subjects participating in experiments due to the inevitable heightened tension at certain procedural intervals—but the current experiment's difficulties had yet to manifest. So Ronny—what had come over him? How could the gossip in the park have caused such melodrama? Had he misjudged Ronny? If Ronny jumped ship—he glanced at Paul, still paused at the equipment cabinet, where he'd been since Ronny barged in—Paul would step in on Ronny's behalf, the Doctor felt sure. The test must not be hindered due to any human error or weakness or character flaw. The test was infallible. But Ronny—

"Son," the Doctor started, "we have no time for gossip, forget what you think you heard, I refuse to have—rumors—disrupt our work, Ronny, understand?"

"Excuse me, Doc, because—" Paul started to say something.

The Doctor nodded and extended his arm as if to usher Paul's interjection into the room.

"The test flight isn't scheduled for a couple more weeks, correct?"

The Doctor nodded, felt at his breast pocket for a pen.

"Then Ron, why don't you go back home for the rest of the day, sleep it off? You won't miss anything crucial this afternoon—nothing we can't fill you in on," Paul said.

"Yes, why not," the Doctor agreed.

Ronny shook his head. He knew there was a problem. He tried again.

"I think you need to consider, really consider, on the off chance what I heard out there—"

The Doctor had run out of patience.

"The talk happens all the time, Ron, certainly we know I don't win popularity contests around here. But we can't sabotage this based on hearsay—we remain on course. I agree with Paul, take the afternoon off. Tomorrow morning, before dawn, I expect all of us to arrive prepared for business, and Ron, I expect you will think over our work here and come tomorrow refocused. And forget about what you think you heard. Forget it."

And just like that the Doctor dismissed him. Now what, Ronny wondered. If they wouldn't listen—

He knew they were in trouble. He knew it was already too late.

Of course she ran. And by the time she made it to the road that would take her back to the trailer, she slowed to a jog, unsure if Richard Santiago was after her. She pictured him in a golf cart, squirreling down the gravel—and realized that wasn't out of the question. Vivian panicked and crossed to the other side, jogging off into the gully a ways, eventually turning onto a path that appeared to run parallel but actually carved farther into the scraggy woods. She meant to be just out of sight from the road, but soon she was way out of sight, somewhere else, and there was a strange banner in the distance; a looming white rectangle; a white wall. The larger the white wall became until she stood at its base: a willowy canvas screen, a hole punched in the upper right corner but otherwise taut enough, strung on a warped frame. A huge white sail in the trees. She couldn't get any closer; the thick brush bridged like lattice, the roots knotted with weeds. She'd reached an impasse. She took stock of the land. Weeds that groped to three feet in places; jutting elbows of blackthorn; vines tangled around old steel posts.

Three, five, eight, eleven of them. Fifteen, eighteen, they marked a vague grid, speaker posts that had outlasted decades of drought and yard-sale swim trunks and metal detectors. Vivian took in the wrecked surroundings, decrepit and overgrown, and felt like shit after everything: her mother's depressing trailer, Ronny's leaving, not having enough money for the ashes. And how did everything go wrong, anyway. What was the first collapse, the fracture that ramparted poorly? That there would be no need for a service for her mother. That hardly any relics of her life—besides the hoarded junk—remained and she had, in the end, barely anyone to be remembered to. Vivian thought of something from the letters: *I am building the machine that will conduct an energy of distortions and I have saved the old microwaves for this purpose.* The energy of distortions. Everything was distorted here, in the new days. And Vivian alone at a useless ghost-forest drive-in. She waded out to the midfield, away from the screen, where the brush was looser and surrounded by sand and the posts had turned furry with rot.

She surveyed the land and knew, in a split second, what needed to be done. Richard Santiago was out of luck. It was already late afternoon, the darkness lowering; she was taking too long. Vivian opened the lid of the canister, unfolded the plastic overwrap, and forced herself to look at the powdered gray flakes, the speckled newsprint dust. Ashes were ashes, were soot practically; shadows and pressed carbon atoms. Dust to dust. She opened the bag and counted quickly, and her heart continued to pound, fists of blood knocking loud and knocking louder. Vivian took the open container of her mother's ashes and, tipping it, she jogged the field, scattering the fine powder over that agrestic, disinherited ground. The ashes caught the crisp winter air like filaments of a dandelion clock blown apart and carried.

Though he'd grown up practically right across the street, standing in the backyard of Helen and Paul's house was as good as standing in some random neighborhood in Michigan he'd never set foot in before. Even though he could still gauge exactly where the bike path met up behind the dry cleaners, an eighth of a mile past the high school. It didn't matter where you stood in that town, you could always map your past to your present by the high school and the bike paths.

Out of cigarettes, he went back inside. Paul was staying at the Doctor's house, so there was no way he'd show up at his and Helen's own house—he couldn't risk it—but Ronny still felt strange being there now that Paul was alive and well and twenty minutes away at the most. But Ronny wasn't in the mood to go to his father's house, wasn't in the mood for anything, so he hid out at Paul's and Helen's place, took stock of the nature—three plants dead, four more dying; opened and shut the refrigerator door; took in the mail. Not much happened in a semi-abandoned house, apparently. Dust collected. Bills collected. He drank a beer while he sorted junk from bills from personal stuff. Most of it was junk. He tossed the real mail on the table behind the couch and left the rest in a pile for the trash.

The room was just as it had been that last night Ronny and Vivian had spent there. The night he'd wanted to tell Vivian about the Doctor's master plan; the night she got the news about her mother. The Detox book he'd taken from the shelf and left on the floor, the drinking glass left on the mantle, slicked over wine staining the tumbler. That was the last time he'd been inside, and the way the room was still set up so casual . . . and now he'd returned and everything was still fucked up. Fucked up even worse, kind of, because here he was on the outs with the Doctor, and Paul whom he'd never even met before that day, and his own father, and Vivian, even, maybe, since he still hadn't called though he'd promised he would and had meant to, and by now a whole two days had passed. He was feeling exactly as disengaged as the counselor's color wheel determined an arsonist should be, plotting his next *ignition of sound property* with the intent to *destroy or otherwise harm a person, a place, or a person's material goods*, an act from which one *so afflicted derived great pleasure*. Man, that counselor would love to get his hands on Ronny's current disengagement, graph it, and file it inside his plastic binder.

He decided to search the bedroom, or maybe the office, for a joint. As he headed upstairs, an envelope on the mantle caught his attention. It looked like a personal letter. It was addressed to Paul and it appeared to have been sent during the time he was officially missing. Ronny opened it; he didn't even hesitate, but it was practically split at one corner anyhow. On a sheet of graph paper an early drafting of the wing diagram was penciled in and footnoted with a few equations, an asterisk, and the name of—it looked like a pharmaceutical name, but he couldn't make it out completely, *esevra*-something. Was it possible? That the Doctor had mailed his classified plan through the regular post to the house of a missing person, addressed to the missing person—actually, who could say, maybe that was genius. Maybe the Doctor was so fucking brilliant he would pull this off after all. In the meantime, one man was no longer missing and the wings had yet to be tested. There was bound to be a convergence. He couldn't believe he had waited so long—he had to call Vivian.

Last night, in the final hours of the new century, two days, seven hours and thirteen minutes before the war began, she sat in the rocker by the window in the room they said was hers, that looked out over a courtyard scaped with marigolds and pebbles, and remembered half-remembered pieces of her long life: dust rising on a midway that stretched through weathered tents; a damp afternoon on the ferry over the Baltic Sea; a forest knotted over with stumps and vining undergrowth; running through a winter night; a burning house; his hand on her bare shoulder; the dark take of sleep.

When Vivian returned to the trailer, night had already consumed the shape of things to blue black; the stars were grim. Seth was assembling an awkward contraption out of clocks and radios, TV antennas and something busted that resembled a toy keyboard—probably a toy keyboard—and a scroll of chicken wire. He consulted a notebook as he adjusted one of the radio bodies.

"What's that?" Vivian pointed.

Seth handed her the notebook.

She read the writing scrawled across the top margin: *Mission operative communication assemble as pictured below.*

"Plans?" she said. Seth nodded.

She flipped a few pages and tossed the notebook to the floor where Seth hunched over a taped-together arm of wires. What she wondered was: what was Seth's deal. Did he recognize the strangeness of their diminished universe? Or did he not analyze the state of things, generally? Despite how mostly normal he seemed to her, the fact that he didn't speak caused Vivian to think of him as existing in an alternate dimension. That night, in that moment, he looked like an overgrown boy sitting there on the floor, like a man playing with toys. She was disgusted, suddenly, and exhausted, and felt her voice rising before she even knew what she'd said.

"This is fucked up, Seth."

He looked up, startled.

"No, listen—why are you building that? It's not a real machine, it's not anything, it's nonsense, for Christ's sake, it's not actually going to do anything, do you get that? Do you get that it's a fucking *joke*, a fucking sad and fucked-up joke? Do you?"

She had become furious and felt out of control. This place was making her sick. The neutral, Band-Aid colored paneling; the low ceiling; the neurotic machinery pilfered from Sister Agnes' Helping Hand's dumpster. She felt how crippling the trailer was right then, how much of a burden it would be to take responsibility for its contents, and for the stifling arrangement of its fake walls, and the Plexiglas window over the sink, and the depressing kitchenette—realized that she had, without knowing it, been contemplating moving in.

Vivian threw her hands up in exasperation—wanting to throw something, smash something against the wall—and flung them stupidly, cartoonish, done.

"*What* is *wrong* with you?" she said. "You can't even talk."

She had almost succeeded in not saying it, but Seth had already turned back to carefully wrapping the coil of wire over the adapter, not even paying attention, and she couldn't help herself. And then it was too late and she was shouting at him.

"You're turning into her—you joined the *circuit* for fuck's sake! Did you forget how much she hated that life? What is wrong with you? It's like you live inside your own pathetic universe just like her, that's what she did! Why would you do that to yourself? What the fuck is the point?"

There was nothing to do to take it back, and she had started to cry but she said it anyway, "It's embarrassing, how you are, and you don't have a fucking clue."

Seth froze, as if he was too shocked to know what to do at first, as if surprised she could be cruel. She couldn't do anything either; she just stood there, unable to move as Seth finally collected himself, stood up—the fury rising, clenching his jaw and reddening his face—and slammed his hand through the wall behind him, then knocked past Vivian, shoving her hard out of the way. He was outside, having shut the door so forcefully it bounced back open, by the time she realized that he hadn't actually hit her, she'd just thought he would.

The next day, and the day after, and the day after passed, no sign of Seth. She wondered if he'd gone to the neighbors—surely he had gone to the neighbors and would be back before too long. So she only half-looked in the woods every time she hauled more junk out to the yard. No sign of him. When the phone finally rang by the end of the second day, Vivian answered quickly, relieved, sure it would be the neighbors telling her Seth was on his way back from their farm.

"Vivian, listen, I'm sorry," Ronny rushed into his apology while Vivian stared at the grooves in the paneling, ran her thumb up and down the dusty gap.

"I'm sorry I waited until tonight, but things here—"

Something in her body fluttered, rising to the surface, magnetized at his voice, but—then where the hell was Seth.

He was saying, "Vivian, I have news besides—"

When she heard Paul's name she snapped to attention as if from a daze; she had no idea what Ronny had said just before or after but on Paul's name everything stopped.

"What?" she said.

"He's back. He's here, but not exactly what you're—wait, hold on."

Maybe he took a swig of something. She heard him swallow, or cough, some slight wave in his throat.

"He's back," Ronny said again, "but he's not supposed to be back in the way we thought, um expected, and I found a letter here at the house . . ."

That sounded vaguely familiar to Vivian.

". . . anyway, I opened it. It was sent from the Doctor to Paul, and had instructions, you know, some information about the project, which I told you about, the wings, but he showed up at the lab this morning. I fucking met him, because he was there to help the Doctor, because he has been all along."

"He was missing."

"Hiding out. Not missing."

"And Helen—"

"Doesn't know. No idea. There's no way."

"That he's back?"

"Doesn't know he's alive or not officially, never officially, missing. No. None of it."

Vivian felt oddly defeated. Duped. What she'd been shuffling around in that big house was not catastrophe, but run of the mill. That poor wife.

There was no more room for small talk after that. Ronny tried. Said how are you, how is Seth, has it snowed the first good snow. She didn't tell him Seth was gone; didn't tell him what she'd done. Didn't tell him what she was going to do. She wanted to. But she couldn't bear to acknowledge any of it, and what would he say if she did.

"Everything's fine here Ronny," she said. "We're all fine."

The first good snow had not yet fallen, but the chill in the wind was more severe, cut closer to the bone, the days since Seth was gone. You wouldn't last out there. She could call the neighbors. She half dialed, hung up. Where he'd punched the wall, the paneling had split through, allowing the cold air to press in more efficiently and drop the temperature a whole degree. There was a space heater that almost replaced as much warmth as was lost, but it smelled like burning and was only a temporary solution. Things were stopping. First the phone service would get shut off. The water would go next; then the electricity. The notices accumulated. The bills changed from white to blue, orange, yellow, each color a more urgent warning. Vivian couldn't make the payments, her mother had let the bills lapse for weeks before she died. Suddenly she felt overwhelmed by all the bland versions of giving in to mediocre options that a decrepit single-wide musters up in its rural isolation. All the waning options.

There were still some cartons to go through, some drawers. It made sense to fake investigate the contents while she waited for Seth to return. Still, there was no way to redeem her actions if he did. She'd taken the machine away from him, ridiculed it, when all it did was measure the rate at which something was lost. That contraption, that machine he was building, was their mother, if you thought about it the way Seth probably did. But all Vivian could think was: that made her an alien. She pulled files from the remaining boxes and started to read.

Maps and warranties. Calendars defaced with excessive plans that corresponded to things she remembered from the conspiracy letters—*We must be prepared to conquer the forces*. Newspapers from Roswell. Addresses for the Center for AI board members. And then, in the fourth box, there were two snapshots. One showed her young grandparents in their bathing suits, smiling wide smiles, standing on a dirt midway next to a small man, barefoot, cigar in his mouth and capuchin monkey on his shoulder. The monkey's tail curled around his arm. One showed her mother as a child—it had to be her mother, no question, that squint, that wavy hair—playing in the dirt in puffy bloomers, knees scratched, sitting in front of a sandwich board that was painted with big loops: 20 CENTS LIVE SHOW. She turned them over, hoping to find her grandmother's handwriting, but if anything had been written on the backs of the photos, even a date, it had faded a long time ago. Vivian put the photographs aside, and pulled out something else, realizing this was the box that contained everything she was afraid to find. She unfolded the paper from its oversized envelope: a birth certificate.

Evangeline Marie Foster, the blanks filled in, *Born in Cleveland, OH*, her quavery signature, *Gave birth to Seth Everett Foster on this twelfth day of March, 1974, at 8:29 a.m. EST, Saint of the Blizzard Hospital, in the town of Russia, in the state of North Carolina.* Black marker struck the father's name. She held up the certificate to the overhead light: nothing. To the mini-light over the mini-stove: almost. Vivian could almost make out the first letter of the first name. Then she noticed that the father's place of birth hadn't been marked out. He'd been born in Ireland. Reddingshire. One more detail than she'd ever had. But she wasn't surprised or elated, she was amassing facts from a vantage point that felt vastly, oceanically removed, like how somewhere far away a glacier was shrinking by the dust of Antarctica's low-lying clouds. A seizure of mass that would take years to register.

She went through the rest of the box quickly, intent on locating her own certificate, the other half. It wasn't until she made it through the next box and a half that she found it. Filed between a *National Geographic* circa 1987 on Lithuania, and a *Satellite Sally Satellites for Women Beginner's Manual. Evangeline Marie Foster, born in Cleveland, OH*, quavery signature, *Gave birth to Vivian Merritt Foster on this twelfth day of March,*

1974, at 8:33 a.m. EST, Saint of the Blizzard hospital, in the town of Russia, in the state of North Carolina. Father's name, a black mark. A name given, a name taken. So they'd never get to know. They'd only have her, no one else, nothing else.

All this time, her whole life, really, she'd never wondered much about her father. The family she did have had always seemed far away, and distant, even when they were right there, living in the same apartment—it had never occurred to her to want an additional family member who was even more of a stranger, a stranger several times removed; why bother? But that night, holding the birth certificate, seeing the blacked-out name, she wondered. Probably because this was it. The only piece left that remained unknown.

With a flashlight she could almost make out three separate names, and the first looked like . . . Frampton. She turned it over, and turned it upside down, and it did, it looked like Frampton, again and again, Frampton, after thirty minutes it was still Frampton . . . E-something . . . no, C maybe, there was an L or T, or H. Dawn was breaking when she looked again, upside down, one last time, and decided, after an entire night, there was only one name possible under the smear of black ink: Frampton Colton O'Connell.

The next morning, Vivian dialed the operator.

"What listing?"

She had written it down: *Frampton Colton O'Connell. Frampton C.* She cleared her throat. She gave the full name of the party. The operator put her on hold. Vivian waited, wanting it over with. The operator clicked back over.

"Miss? I have a Franklin O'Connell in Lincoln and an F.C. O'Connell in Grand City. These were the only matches. Most recent is from 1987."

"F.C. O'Connell, please."

The recorded number came over the line. She had to call back for the reverse listing: 14 North Somerset Avenue, Grand City, Nebraska.

The earliest bus to Grand City was 6:45 the next morning. So she woke before sunrise and she dressed in her warmest clothes, plus Pete's coat and two layers of socks. It took her twenty-five minutes to walk to the station. She bought a ticket with the money she hadn't paid Richard Santiago, and took a seat on one of the benches. Ten minutes later an old man arrived in the station, sat down near her and paged noisily through a newspaper. A broken pink comb fell from his back pocket to the station floor.

The bus approached, gears downshifting abruptly. She took a middle seat, one of many empty, and slid across the cracked vinyl to the window. While she waited for the bus to pull away from the station, Vivian reached for half an abandoned newspaper a few seats up, flipped through—sports, business, classifieds—no obits, which were missing along with all the other sections. She napped, restlessly; woke to a baby's wailing, pitched cry; an hour and a half had passed. She began to wish the town was even farther west, farther away to get to, feeling sick to her stomach with the idea of arriving. Of course she couldn't just call Frampton O'Connell—she had to stake the place out. But she didn't have a plan, besides walking to the address. She wasn't going to knock at the door and make any type of announcement. She wasn't going to introduce herself or, if the house was empty, she wasn't going to break in.

Clouds streamed by, treetops chiseled out parts of the gray. Dry heat forced up through the bus vents, stuttering, electric heat, fogged the windows up against the bitter cold. You cleared the window; it fogged right over. The bus stopped once and a middle-aged man boarded. The bus was moving again, the loud strain and pull, and thirty-five minutes later Vivian got off, followed by a mother with her baby and an elderly couple. She bought a map and sat down, shuffled the awkward rectangle open. All the downtown streets followed a basic grid of parallel lines. Easy enough, she thought, locating Somerset Avenue as a road threading off the major stretch, and she began the forty-minute trek to the other side of town.

She walked briskly, past brick buildings with lawyer or dentist or insurance placards. A tattoo parlor, a post office. A grocer. Another block: a butcher, a chiropractor, a tropical fish outlet. Another block: she did not have a reunion in mind. She did not go bearing news. Another block: would he want to know her mother was dead? Another block: was it her responsibility to tell him? Past warehouses, restaurant supply stores. The town fell away to open spaces, the streets kept stretching out, sprawling landmarks by a mile, Dairy Queen, Gas Station, Center for Family Planning. A few cars, a few vans, a parking lot eventually, a liquor store, a mechanic, a strip club. The street Vivian needed would branch off any minute, because her road had become a legitimate highway. And there was Salt Lick, and Salt Lick turned into Rosemary, and Rosemary forked into Evergreen and Evergreen dead-ended at Somerset.

Vivian followed Somerset, a two-lane road, half a mile—it was cold but she walked quickly, didn't care, didn't notice—a strip of shops lined up to the right, a small access road—she stopped, drank from her canteen—actually, she felt a bit feverish—and followed Somerset to the perimeter, behind the shopping center. Followed it past, waiting for the road to veer off residentially—split-levels, yards, bikes—another mile, another half mile, and then the only activity was a farm, fenced in cattle and a silo: 21 North Somerset.

Vivian had passed 14 North Somerset, somehow, without seeing a neighborhood, an apartment building, a single house. She felt her adrenaline thinning. There was nothing to do but walk back to the access road and ask at one of those shops, provided they weren't deserted. It had only been an hour since she left the station; an hour was a manageable distance. She adjusted her bag to the other shoulder and started back. A truck honked at her as it sped by.

After about fifteen minutes, she saw the concrete backbone of the shopping center up ahead and felt relieved that she'd made progress by reaching a half-familiar landmark. Taking a detour into the weak arrangement of woods, Vivian clomped through brambles and trash and emerged on the other side, an expanse of asphalt and dried oil stains but no cars. She faced a discount department store with a FIFTY PERCENT OFF flag in every window and a clearance banner above the entrance. The lot number of the discount department store was 10. She scanned the cigar shop next door for its number: 11. Next to that a diner, the only place that appeared mildly operational: 12 N. Somerset. The hardware store had to be 13 and that would make 14 an adult bookstore. A neon XXX branded the small window over the door. Fourteen North Somerset was an adult bookstore called Triple X. It wasn't open, and there was a No Trespassing notice taped to the door. But it was the correct address, that was undeniable. Beneath the No Trespassing sign black stickers spelled it out. Fourteen North Somerset Avenue. Fuck.

Wedged in a few doors down, forming the crook of the U, was a place called Snappers. Aside from being confused, Vivian was starting to get pissed off, because what kind of shitty deal was this. How could the operator's address for F.C. O'Connell match Triple X?

There was a payphone outside Snappers. Vivian fished some dimes and the scrap of paper with F.C. O'Connell's number out of her bag. She slid the coins down the throat of the box, heard the dial tone register, and dialed; messed up and had to start again. The phone was silent after she pressed the seventh digit, and then the delayed ring, long-lasting and echoey. Another ring and another ring, she was counting them. At nine she knew no one was going to answer or they already would have. At sixteen she knew the answering machine wasn't going to click on, if there was one, but she stayed on the line, counted twenty-two, counted twenty-four. At twenty-nine a pick-up pulled into the lot. Thirty. It circled slowly. She stayed on the phone, thirty-one, and in three more rings the truck pulled back out to the main road, squealing its tires, and the phone was ringing thirty-five, and the phone was ringing thirty-six.

A skirt of flame, smoke plumes petticoating wide, roaming, layer after layer of fire trembling the dark forest, a floating furnace that illuminated the dead pinetops then felled them in swift collapse. The smoke coarsened room, coarsened lung, and mapped over the dwindling hours with embers and ash. The wildfires raged, and those who refused to evacuate sipped bottled water and locked their doors. Morning was an ugly country no one dared to name.

The ride back was a brief intermission of fitful sleep. Her body registered the halts and shiftings of the bus and the movements of other passengers boarding, de-boarding. She kept her eyes closed. The ride back was the exact same journey minus all of the original anticipation. The speaker crackled the names of towns through static, one by one, until the last stop was Valentine. She wandered out into the waning dusk and somehow made it back to the trailer, though she never even remembered walking out of the station. She woke the next day, and began again.

The note from Seth said he'd gone back to the circuit. Said *Sorry about the wall.* Said *I'm in Vegas so's Melody.* Said *Goodbye Viv. I'm sorry I made you mad I didn't mean to be an asshole.*

The bird was squawking in the other room. She thought it was good that Seth had returned to his affairs. To his livelihood. To his girlfriend, Melody, the miniature horse trainer. She thought that she wanted to think it was good, the life he'd invented. It was hard to measure from there. Hard to know one thing. At least, she thought, he was accounted for. And though when he left she'd resigned herself to the distance between them, a failure on her behalf, for sure—still, it meant that there was no reason not to get on with things. And about what must be done, Vivian was certain. She knew what she was going to do.

First, though, she took the whiskey from the cabinet. Ronny had discovered the stash. She drank what was left of the bottle, a warmth that stung, that sank from her throat to her stomach to her bones and anchored. She crouched on the kitchen floor, already feeling the sour rising. She never wanted to move again. Wanted to forget the body's ability to recognize other bodies, like a magnet; other bodies' warmths; other openings and closings; the flush; the air in the lungs; that apparatus of hush and heat; that fever, that heaving. Vivian sat as still as she clumsily could that afternoon, drunk and waiting for the phone to ring. She pictured Ronny rolling a cigarette, his fingers smoothing the paper, meticulous and steady. She wanted him to call, wanted his voice to brace her to something better, something firm, but the phone didn't ring. She finally passed out, and she was hundreds of miles away.

For the next ten hours, she slept. And half-slept. Nothing registered fully—a dog barking far off, a deep shadow closing over the room—then finally the commotion of someone standing over her, shaking her arm, trying to get to her through the fog. Vivian squinted at the orthopedic shoe, white laces double-knotted.

"Dear?"

Mrs. Randall's face was peering down at her. The rings on her fingers were shiny and heavy looking. Vivian sat up, tried to think of why Mrs. Randall would be there.

"Dear I hate to wake you, I just wanted to stop by and check in, I tried phoning but I just . . . well, you've been here all alone."

So she did know that Seth had left. Vivian nodded, scanned the place: boxes still towering haphazardly, junk scattered, faulty mechanisms everywhere.

"You know, I was worried when you didn't answer. Well, I guess I just think the worst now, afraid I will for some time, I," she stopped there and stood in the middle of the junk, wringing her hands at the mess. "What will you . . . do . . . with this," she said, peering around the contents of the trailer as if prepared to be frightened by what might jump out of a larger box. "Have you given any thought to . . . what you might like to do with this—place? She did own it? I'm sure you— "

Vivian shook her head and said, "I haven't really thought about it."

"It would be a shame," she went on, as if Vivian hadn't spoken, or hadn't understood what she'd meant by the question, "to lose your mother's investment, Vivian."

She nodded politely. All she wanted to do was destroy it. It was making her tired, talking like this to the last person who knew her mother before she died, pretending there was anything important that had to be done with the trailer, anything that had to do with investments. It was doubtful there was an insurance policy. It didn't need to exist anymore, and no one could accuse her of collecting anything off it.

Mrs. Randall absently lifted a yellow newspaper from the stack on the table, ruffled the dry leaves of it, put it back down. "Well. If you need anything," she said, making her way back to the door. "Do you have enough clothes? Do you have a scarf? You're warm enough here?"

"I'm fine," Vivian said. "I just have a headache, that's all."

She was still huddled on the couch, cross-legged. It occurred to her that she was being impolite, inhospitable, that she should offer to make some tea, but she couldn't bring herself to suggest it. She didn't want to pretend not to see the look that would flash across Mrs. Randall's face as she hesitated, wondering how dirty the teacups were. Vivian didn't bother trying.

The cold air rushed in as Mrs. Randall opened the door, and Vivian crossed her arms against her chest. "I'm fine," she said again as Mrs. Randall pursed her lips and half-nodded. From the doorway, the neighbor surveyed the trailer one more time then turned back into the winter night, letting the aluminum door snap shut.

Dormant field; moonlight spindled through dead branches. The air, dense and cold before the snow. Vivian put the bird in a shoebox nested with phone book pages and a sweatshirt sleeve. Tucked the box at the edge of the drive, then walked back, the matchbook in her sweaty hand. She struck one, counted the paces it took to extinguish as she approached the trailer. Four. She'd have to get closer to start with, then run. She lit another and held it burning a few seconds, a flare. Bending down slowly, she held the tip out as far as possible, arm's length, between two fingers. Not steady enough. It went out. She lit a third, knelt down to the edge of the trailer by the side of the porch steps where she'd stacked boxes of newspapers. Those would take. She touched the match to the paper. Nothing happened. She held it there, pressing, and after a full minute it started to smolder.

She should have used gasoline and just torched it, and suddenly she realized it might not work. She lit another match, dropped it into the box, and there was, right away, a gathering sound, a rustling into motion sound, a quickening, then a pop as the box's sheaf of dried paper bloomed into a swathe of fire. As fast as she could, Vivian struck another match, wedged it into the splint of the step where the wood was peeling away, then another match, then another, then tossed the whole book onto the fire, took three large steps backward, and ran. It was small, but it was building.

She looked back once, when she got to the road that led out to the bus station. Couldn't see much from there, maybe a faint glow, like a campfire seen from a great distance. Or maybe she saw nothing at all but the black woods. She wrapped the box with the bird in it between her bulky coat arms, not sure it would do much good, and started the long walk to the station, sure that any second the sirens would churn through the wilderness and she would be arrested.

In the station's restroom, she made sure the bird was alive. It was squashed in a corner and trembled. She unspooled a bunch of paper towels and tucked them over the nest. Went back out to buy a ticket east, one way. Twenty-seven minutes, the guy said. Slid the ticket across. She didn't think about what she'd done. Bus 79 pulled into the station at approximately 9:34 p.m. Most of the passengers' compartment lights stayed on overhead, and that felt comforting to Vivian for some reason, less lonely. She tried to sleep but couldn't stop herself from picturing the trailer on fire, the smoke trailing in columns, pulling into the sky, and she wondered for the first time what would happen when the neighbors found out. What would they think—that she'd died in the fire, or escaped, or started it? Her mother's investment. Vivian wondered what the odds were that the trailer would burn itself out, that the next morning there would be a rough patch of waning, sluggish embers that would just die out, no big deal, no big crime, no need to investigate. She felt sick to her stomach as it dawned on her that she hadn't actually thought through these parts of her plan. She'd just done the only thing that made sense to her to do. In the patchy light, sitting there on the bus, she ached from missing Ronny. And Seth, even, and even her mother. And she wanted to confess to Ronny, tell him what she'd started. He was the only person she could think of who might understand. And if he didn't, he would at least convince her that she wasn't a terrible person, which she was starting to doubt, because the evidence was mounting against her. She took the photographs out of her knapsack, where she'd stowed them, and studied them in the intermittent flashes of neon lights from gas pumps and liquor stores the bus sped past. Her grandparents looked so joyful posing there on the sandy fairgrounds. If they knew their daughter was miserable, would they have left that life behind, or would they have stayed anyway, and let her mother go?

Two hours later, something was wrong. They'd stopped moving. Beyond the bus windows, deep drifts of snow wedged the highway into a narrow strip of white.

A voice called out into the darkness, "What are we, broke down?"

The bus driver addressed the bus from the pitch-black aisle, "No reason to panic, folks. Just a situation with the engine. Of course, as you'll notice, the weather's getting downright treacherous, so—" he sighed, not eager to admit it, "—we're going to have to stop for the night. I've called some arrangements in, van's gonna transport us to town, up a few more miles, not far, and we'll stay the night. I'm going to have to ask you to remain seated until the van arrives. Appreciate your patience, folks."

He sat back down. Radioed something over to Central.

When the van arrived it was long past midnight, and the snow had resumed. The passengers stumbled off the bus and crowded onto the van, luggage piled onto knees, braced under wet shoes. The roads were icy, the eight-mile drive to the motel painstakingly slow. In the frozen early morning, in the wood-paneled lobby, the passengers stood on line at the check-in desk and the clerk rebooted his computer for the second time.

Vivian stood in the dim hallway, working the key. The panel of fluorescent lighting flickered above her head, equal parts shadow. Heavy wool curtains on the window: large pineapples on damask dragged stiffly to the floor. The dial on the radiator was hard to adjust. When the heat cut on, the steam rattled until it bellowed up the walls. The bird chirped, the first sound she'd made in hours, and Vivian didn't know how much longer Picnic would bear the circumstances. She was puffy and not moving. Poor bird. Vivian folded a towel over the radiator and put the box on top. She left the light on. Her goal was to fall into a shallow, uneventful half-sleep for the few short hours she had before it would be time to reboard the bus. Instead, she slipped immediately into an agonizing dream in which she set the trailer on fire not realizing that both her mother, who was alive again, and Seth were inside. They were trapped, and as the trailer started melting into flames, their screams got louder, and Vivian's legs were stone, she was helpless to move or try to put the fire out and the flames shot higher, consuming the night sky. She woke up in a cold sweat, not sure she was alive.

The bird didn't make it through the night. Vivian gingerly wrapped Picnic in a pillowcase and returned her to the box. She did not want to leave the dead bird in her motel room, so she carried the box outside. Across the parking lot there was a stretch of land and some pines, but the ground was frozen. There was no way to dig a decent hole. Vivian went around to the edge of the lot where manicured shrubs lined the property. Reaching far back to the drooping, snow heavy boughs, she shoved the box underneath. The branches fell back into place, draping the small coffin with its underbrush. It was crummy, even if it was the best place she could think of, out of the whole motel grounds, and she felt genuinely sorry for not managing better for the bird. That was not how she would have preferred things go. Back in her room, she paced the gross mauve carpet—cigarette marks, large water stains circling out from the radiator, limp folds near the chest of drawers—until the new bus pulled in.

The little roads that led back to the main highway were hardly plowed, just sanded over. The first hour was unbearable, the bus laboring to tread the ground, plow forward. Her jaw ached from clenching her teeth. The roads were lousy, and the sky gave no promise that it wouldn't snow again, a gray curtain folding over the tree tops and power lines.

"Eat, no, we'll eat when we get home, baby," she heard a woman say a few rows back. Two kids played in the aisle with checkers, clattered them down with their fists. They reminded Vivian suddenly, terribly, of Seth. Crouched on the floor, trying to build that machine like a little kid playing with his chemistry set. He had completely shut himself off, refusing to communicate except in his elementary charades; he just didn't get it, any of it. But then why hadn't he defended himself when she'd yelled at him? She'd been horrible to him, and made him angry, but he hadn't tried to change her mind. He just punched the wall and went away. How could they be twins? What had ruined their mother, she feared, was ruining him. Unless it was ruining her. An apple rolled from the back of the bus, scattering the black and red coins under the seats before the kids' small hands could rescue them.

The bus shuddered its way to the next station, the end of the line, as it started to rain. There, Vivian would board another bus that would take her the rest of the way. Her voice was so hoarse from not talking the operator had to ask her name twice before the collect call could be authorized.

"Vivian?" Ronny sounded strange, and she couldn't tell if he was happy to hear from her. Her stomach sank. When Vivian had decided to call, she had guessed Ronny would be at Paul and Helen's house, and hoped he might pick up if he was, but mainly she'd called Helen's house because it was the only number she knew.

"What's wrong," Ronny said, "what?"

"Nothing, no, I just got off a bus, I just got here, I."

She stopped, didn't know what she was doing. Even if it was a mistake, she didn't have any other option. She didn't even have money for a taxi.

"Where are you?"

"At the bus depot from St. Louis. I have to catch another bus in a few minutes. I thought—"

"You're coming back here? Viv, tonight?"

"Ronny," the announcement overhead drowned out her words, "I did something terrible."

"Viv, you're on your way back? Do you—I'm going to meet you at the station, Viv. St. Louis? Don't go anywhere, don't walk home, just tell me when your bus gets in."

More announcements blared overhead, cutting off whatever came next.

Ronny repeated something but Vivian had already hung up.

Finally, a little after midnight, the bus pulled into the station, and Vivian was back where she'd started. It felt like a year had passed, though she'd only been gone a little over two weeks. Here she was at the end of the line. She was nervous about seeing Ronny, and even more nervous that he might not show up, but he was there as promised, smoking near the entrance.

"Welcome back," he said in greeting. He reached out, touched the collar of Pete's coat with his fingertip. She leaned into him without thinking, and felt his body resist on impulse before giving in and pulling her tightly to him, and pressing his lips softly to her forehead. Tears welled in her eyes, hot. They stood like that for a minute or two, until Ronny broke the embrace gently, guiding her over to the car.

The Dasher smelled like the drive out to Valentine, pavement and stale smoke and damp upholstery—windows left down in multiple rainstorms and dried out again, sun-cracked vinyl, musty ventilation. They drove in silence until they neared the high school, where Ronny pulled into the lot and parked the car. Before Vivian could ask what they were doing there, Ronny said, "Vivian, I have to tell you something."

When the Doctor had risen to the dark morning, preparing for the long day ahead, he had not envisioned disaster on this scale. What on earth had happened? What had gone so wrong? If this was Ronny's attempt to instill whatever point—but no, no, it was easy to see this installment—whoever was responsible—meant business. The chains around his lab door officially locked him out. His face burned with anger and soon his neck burned beneath his collar, causing him to feel constricted. He kicked the door as an afterthought, not hard enough. There was a posted notice above the doorknob: No Trespassing. The Doctor quickly turned—how brutal the embarrassment if his colleagues spied him there, puzzled and lurking, locked out of his own room—and headed to the back entry, where there might be a chance—

The office of Dr. Shirsdon abutted his own, which meant the rooms were connected by a shared storage closet, though they never employed that conduit as a passageway. Each secured his closet door, but it was purely out of respect for the other's space. Dr. Shirsdon was a middle-aged orthopedic surgeon, thankfully not overly engaged in hospital politics and most likely not even aware of the Doctor's mounting reputation. Most likely. And there was a possibility, if the Doctor could get into Shirsdon's lab, if that door was unlocked, that he could make it through to his own via the supply closet. He'd crawl through the duct work if he had to. The Doctor took the corner slowly, careful not to encounter anyone. The halls were fairly empty still, since it was barely a minute past five in the morning, but he held his breath in spite of himself as he hurried to the end of the corridor. His hand on the doorknob, he turned—locked. The disappointment was intense. He tried again, in case. Locked. He started down the hall to the exit stairs, breaking into a sweat. He'd made it halfway to the stairs when he heard a door open behind him.

"Doctor, can I help you?"

Dr. Shirsdon was leaning into the hallway.

"Sir, what luck, yes!" The Doctor hurried back, his hands reaching out to shake Shirsdon's arm. "I hoped you might let me through," the Doctor said.

Shirsdon stepped back, let the Doctor follow him inside. "You did not knock," he said, pointedly.

"No, well, I assumed you would not be in so early, but if by chance your door was open . . . see," he ducked his head, not wanting to elaborate, "I'm in a bit of a bind this morning."

Shirsdon leaned against the counter, arms folded, elbow patches visible over pinstripe. He frowned slightly. "Doctor, I must say—if you'll allow me to be so candid, I've overheard some stirrings of late I'm hopeful are simply nonsense. I wouldn't want to believe you were invested in something . . . inadvisable." He looked at the Doctor, who met his gaze reluctantly.

"Yes, I assure you, nonsense is all it is; I've been keeping tabs on some of the least flattering tales myself. No need to worry; I just forgot my key and I'd like to get in a few extra hours this morning, get the preliminaries worked over for Lansing in 732." He nodded brusquely yet collegially to Shirsdon, summoning what pride he could to maintain an air of confidence and neutralize his growing desperation—which he feared was about to give him away. "Now, if you'll excuse me."

Heading off potential questions, the Doctor started to the supply closet cornered on the far side of the room. Once safely inside, in the darkness, he sighed, half-furious and half-relieved, crossing from his side of the closet back into his lab. He locked the door behind him as the scene registered, and he almost passed out.

He couldn't believe it.

They'd gotten in. His files were dumped from their cabinets. The cabinets were overturned. The drawers were flanked open. The papers on which he had mocked up glide and wind resistance diagrams were strewn across the room, fluttered to the floor and over counters. The tablets of graph paper cluttered with penciled dimensions and spatial equations were ripped open haphazardly. The old cards from carnivals and state fairs and sideshows littered the room, ripped from the inner sanctum of the Doctor's hidden panel cabinet. The whole place ransacked. He rummaged through the mess for his blueprint file, looking for the finalized copy with the setup process, all the measurements, ratios of height and weight and harness orientation, but could locate only an early draft. He couldn't breathe adequate breaths and his heart raced. It would have to suffice. He had run out of time.

Everything was coming to an end. Even as the dawn broke. Even as the coffee was poured into cups. Even as the newspaper was spread across the kitchen table. The outside world was encroaching. Paul had pressed play on the answering machine, and between hang-ups and courtesy calls, Helen's message was a brick through the window. *Vivian, hello dear, call me back, just checking in, did you get the check, have you remembered the—*Paul erased it without hearing the reminder. Ronny had brought Vivian in the night before, put her right to bed and left her alone while he guarded the wings in the basement. He and Paul took shifts. The wings spanned a gorgeous arc across the basement floor, threw shadows worthy of an actual swan, bold and scalloped and easily stretching wider than the length of Ronny's arms, fingertip to fingertip.

That morning, Paul and Ronny sat at the kitchen table waiting for the Doctor to arrive. Vivian woke late in the morning and wandered into the room, sat down at the table. She tried not to convey her hostility. But when Ronny introduced her to Paul, she noted that he didn't seem particularly sheepish, sitting there with his sleeves rolled up, casually reading the sports page, pouring more coffee, and she couldn't stop herself from saying it.

"So you're Helen's husband?"

Paul nodded. "Yes," he said, "I am."

"The missing husband . . . whose wife hired me to watch over the house while she hides out in Florida, because her grief is driving her crazy."

Paul put his coffee down hard on the counter and held his hands up saying, "Whoa, hold on, hold on. This has nothing to do with Helen. I love my wife. Did you ever think maybe I was protecting her by keeping her out of the drama— "

Paul paused, shooting a meaningful look at Ronny.

"It's okay," Ronny said. "She knows about it."

Paul started to talk again and Vivian cut him off.

"She hired police to look for you. She's terrified something happened. She drinks all day, then calls begging me for updates." She shook her head. "Look, I'm not going to pretend you're not here. If she calls and I answer the phone . . . "

Paul and Ronny were silent.

"She has no idea, does she?" Vivian asked. Paul shook his head.

"It's not an easy situation," he said quietly.

Vivian stared at the newspaper, eventually flipping to the obituaries and adding up the points in her head.

They drank cup after cup of coffee and said nothing. They turned pages. They considered their luck. They waited for the Doctor to arrive. Everything was coming to an end.

There was not enough time. At most, they had two weeks if they attached the wings immediately. At the absolute minimum, Ronny
would need twelve days of recovery before the test flight. He told
Vivian in the car, in the parking lot, on the way home from the station. "I didn't want to scare you," he told her. "I didn't want you to
have to know." She had punched him in the arm, harder than she'd
meant to, furious. She couldn't believe he was going through with it.
"Are you joking?" She had almost begged him, "Ronny, why? Why on
earth would you—what if it goes wrong? Or if something happens—or, so
what, what if it works? What are you going to do—with permanent fucking
wings?" She was so angry she couldn't even cry. Ronny reached over to
take her hand, but she pulled away from him. "No. I don't understand
how you can do this. I don't understand."

Ronny sighed, trying to figure out how to say it.

"I've thought about it. And I think it's important. I want to—do this
thing that no one else can do—that seems important. Does that make me
an asshole? I don't know. I don't even care anymore. Come on, Vivian!
You understand—what else is there to do? For me?"

Vivian had stared out the window at the senior tennis courts.

"Ronny, what are you going to do with permanent wings? You
won't be able to do anything—I mean, imagine even trying to fucking
drive? With those—"

He sighed, and shrugged, suddenly irritated and tired of talking.

"Sure, things can get complicated, but what's going to be impossible? And I don't fucking care if something's easy or not, because when
was the last time anything was easy around here, Vivian, face it—what is
there to lose that's so great? For me? What is there for me?"

She had tried to picture Ronny, how he would be after, but kept
drawing a blank; all she could conjure was a shadowy, fleeting, angular
shape. And she'd gotten it. He wasn't factoring her in. He wasn't asking.

He was giving her the facts. The streetlamps went on, mapping various archipelagoes of light across the asphalt, and Vivian sat there trying not to say anything else, trying to convince herself to give up.

Now the Doctor was washing his hands, scrubbing them at the kitchen sink. Ronny was strapped to a cot set up by the counter, face down, his view limited to a narrow rectangle of stove and a plaid dishtowel slung over the handle. The IV dripped thickly down the line into his arm, a paper mask over his mouth, a needle in his back as the Doctor numbed the areas where he needed to ladder the bones from his spine. Ronny had seen it: an H-shaped brace, which would act as an extra support to increase the strength of the graft joints. It would be fused on either side of the spine, and the wings would be sutured on top and then adjusted to the correct tension.

The shot was cold and sharp, a sting he felt spread over both shoulders. Ronny tried to make his mind relax along with his slowing-down body. *Where was Vivian?* he thought. Why was he doing this? He knew why, though. He was the only person who could. Where was Vivian? Of course she didn't want to see what was happening. He wondered if there would be a lot of blood. It was awful, being unable to move, strapped down. For some reason he was also unable to speak. He was farther and farther from the room, far away before the knife split through his skin and tugged at his muscles. He was gone long before the Doctor pushed the first shunt into the pocket he'd cut, preparing the graft. By the time the Doctor was asking Paul for a clean towel, Ronny had been asleep for ninety-seven minutes. When he woke, he felt as if his entire body was bruised, as if he'd been pummeled from the inside out. The Doctor leaned over to meet Ronny's glassy eyes. "Son," he said, "You need to rest now."

Before he'd even made sense of the Doctor's words, Ronny's vision went black.

The day had gone fuzzy and hot, so hot he had to continuously wipe the sweat from his forehead. In the distance, flags rippled in the breeze and tents were pitched. In the distance, red, orange and green plastic flags rippled and fluttered in the half-hearted breeze that hardly pushed the heat away, just formed gritty clouds of sand and haze. He walked and walked and walked, struggling to cross the barren expanse to the main tent, which towered over a gathering crowd. Every person carried a covered dish and sported a costume. He got closer and closer—once he had to pause to catch his breath and to drink from the canteen—and finally approached the tent and ducked in, joining a family reunion. His family but not his family, because there was Pete, wearing a suit, fixing a lawnmower, and he could tell Pete was Pete but not his brother, someone else's by now—and there was his mother, by the cliff, carving an enormous boat out of a felled tree trunk with branches scrolling for miles into the distance, you couldn't see where they ended. She was dressed as a sailor and every now and then saluted him. His father rollerskated by, late to the archery range, and there was Evvy, bent over a sewing machine, stitching part of an ocean onto a field—

When he woke he was sweating. Still strapped to the cot, lying on his stomach. He couldn't move, he wanted to roll over. The Doctor was there. Ronny closed his eyes, dizzy and hot from opening them.

The next time he woke it was too dark to see anything in the room. He heard voices though, clips and starts of conversation. Behind him. Nearby. Possibly at the kitchen table. Someone pressed a damp washcloth to his forehead. The dark turned softer.

—Evvy was pulling row after row of ocean through the sewing machine, and he was trying to get to her, trying to run to her, when he noticed the Doctor standing there, pulling gloves over his surgical hands. Before he knew what was happening, Evvy had wings cascading over her shoulders, and when he turned back around he saw Vivian down by the swimming hole, balancing on the rocks, but then she had wings too, and she was floating up into the sky, and again he tried to run but his legs wouldn't work and he was moving very slowly and everyone around him was floating up into the sky, lifted up by their brand-new wings, one by one they drifted up and Ronny shouted to the Doctor but he was drifting away, too, and the sky was going black—

Everything in the room was moving. He couldn't open his eyes.

"Ron," the Doctor said. "You need to wake up now."

He couldn't open his eyes. He couldn't move.

"We're going to get you to stand up now Ron. We're going to help you sit on the edge of the cot first. Let's try opening your eyes. Ron, can you try opening your eyes?"

They felt dry and bloodshot, the light was too bright. The Doctor unstrapped the belts, and gestured for Paul to take the other side. On the count of three they hoisted Ronny up to a sitting position, slowly easing his legs to dangle off the side of the cot. A new rush of pain flashed over his body. He hurt like there was a knife in his shoulder blades, lodging deeper with each shallow breath he managed. The Doctor handed him two red and two blue pills and a paper cup of water, saying, "These will help take the fever down and the pain should start to subside."

It took him a few extra minutes to coordinate the pills on his tongue and the gulp of water that got them down his throat; he was sore all over from the waist up, and weak.

"Ronny, we're going to walk you over to the bedroom now. Get you more comfortable."

When he was on his feet, he thought he would immediately fall down, but Paul grabbed him under his arm and propped him up, hard, steering him over to the hallway.

The wings were heavy, heavier than he'd expected, spread wide, pressed open like soft, atrophied arms folding against the frame of Ronny's shoulders. He couldn't understand them yet. They sort of tipped him forward. They were strange and their burden was awkward, like if your own arms were replaced with hammers or your hands with spades. You'd get used to the heft of a new and useful body part, but non-muscular props like hammers wouldn't automatically respond to sensory impulse as your skin did, as you'd come to expect of it. He felt as if he was wearing scaffolding—the minor part of a bridge—on his back.

When they got him to his room, he was exhausted. "What time is it?" he said, his voice sandpaper. "Where's Vivian?"

The Doctor told him to sleep on his stomach. The dressings were cleaned and changed, and then Ronny felt the bed sheet snag on the outstretched wings as the Doctor lifted the sheet like a sail and let it float down to cover his bulky shape.

"You've been asleep for almost sixty-two hours. You need to keep sleeping for now, and then we have to start to build up your strength, as much as we can, so I'm going to put you on weights. We only have two weeks and—you've done an excellent job, Ron, but the real test—" He didn't finish.

"Where—"

"Vivian's in her room. Now you need to sleep, Ron. We'll be in to check on you every four hours. We'll give you the painkillers and change the dressing but the best thing you can do for yourself is rest."

As the door closed behind him Ronny thought he heard a TV somewhere, loud exclamations filtering over a laugh track. Garish, irrelevant sounds. Ronny wondered if he might be dying.

JUNE 29, 1990

On the morning of the day she died, Vivian Foster woke earlier than usual, woke to dim half-light, slung down clouds fat with impending rain, the shrieking pushcart sounds of the limping bottle collector, the pigeons' scuffed purrs rummaged up from the alley. She woke startled, uneasy, had dreamed that the wings had been sewn into her spine, into her lamina, into her vertebrae. There'd been a mistake. It was supposed to be Ronny up there, but she stood on the bridge, balanced on the steel cable, trying to listen to the Doctor's instructions. She was supposed to jump straight out, as far away from the bridge as possible, but the steel beneath her feet was slick and the fatigue in her body was tremendous.

Twelve days later they gathered in the kitchen. Ronny had managed to shuffle there himself, and leaned gingerly on the back of a chair. The pills the Doctor doled out every four hours were easing all of the tightness he'd felt since the surgery. The spot that was dressed and redressed felt tender. And the wings themselves—he couldn't believe they were a part of him, irreversible and awkward and pulling at the air as he walked sideways down the hall. When he held the mirror up in the bathroom, to catch the reflection above the sink, he almost passed out at the physical impossibility of them, of the sheer, grand reality. They didn't make sense. They weren't his. And yet, something in his brain had already changed, had revised, so when he had the impulse to shift the left wing, the left wing shifted higher, folding into itself as if it was another arm, or an extension of his vertebrae. Or was he imagining that.

Paul stood behind Ronny, applying a thin layer of the tree putty to the wings with a knife, scraping from the inner primary binding to the outer edge, waterproofing. Too little and the wings would soften, depending on humidity; too much and the wings would stiffen and drag, compromising lift.

The Doctor rushed into the kitchen, ready to launch into his emergency broadcast, but paused, abruptly transfixed when he saw Ronny. He reached over, skimmed his finger along the wing's ridge.

"Ron," the Doctor said, "It's magnificent, to see how you are adapting, and how you've healed—magnificent. Ah, Paul, yes, good, good—the wax, time for the wax."

He turned to address the room, hesitating for a second to take note of Vivian, then started in.

"Now, as you know, we don't have any choice," he said. "At nightfall we test. There is no other option. As you know, they raided the lab. Took papers, files, segments of plans certainly. They found everything. Barricaded the room."

The Doctor was different. He had lost his bullying edge; he almost seemed subdued. He looked over at Ronny, who had the crossword a third of the way solved. Twenty-four down: another word for famish.

"Unfortunately, Ron," the Doctor said, "it does appear that you were correct."

Vivian just listened, laying low. She could hardly even look at Ronny. The wings looked more authentic than she'd been prepared for when they were theoretical. There was no way to ignore them, the matted skin that folded and relaxed and made the sound of venetian blinds being pulled up the window or a slick deck of cards shuffled quickly. She couldn't look Ronny in the face. She wondered if she was in mourning, the past week having existentially wasted her. Though she wanted to leave the room, she couldn't budge from the chair. She accidentally kicked Ronny's foot under the table and her apology caught in her throat; she stared at the floor. And she forced herself to listen as the Doctor and Paul and Ronny discussed the intricacies of the new plan, as they considered what to wear, when to meet, where to go, who would charge the walkie-talkies. They required a mountain, but the terrain of the town was flat for hours in all directions; they couldn't drive fast enough to make it to the desired elevation before morning. The buildings were out. No way could they smuggle Ronny and the wings back to campus, through the hospital, up to the forty-ninth floor, now that the Doctor had been banned from the premises—he'd be monitored soon as he set foot in the lobby. Besides the hospital, the other tall buildings in town were less than twenty stories, and they required a technical height of at least one hundred fifty feet to make the mechanics of wingspan and wind lift work. If he couldn't get into the hospital and jump from the observation deck—

"What about the quarry?" Ronny said.

It was deep enough; couldn't even see the bottom of it. As far as getting back out—Paul assured them he had the climbing gear that would hook and pulley to that depth, bring them back up. The men, they had machinery built for excavating and recovery, crane lifts that transport across rugged, precarious rims. Ronny would be fine, the Doctor agreed with Paul. Vivian sat petrified and silent, deliberating her objections. For the love of God, she thought, this plan must be thwarted before Ronny leaped into a quarry and tried to fly with wings sewn into the ribs basketing his body. This triumvirate was absurd. Fuck it.

The Doctor described how the video cameras would operate: one externally with night vision which he himself would control from the quarry's edge (so they had decided then: the quarry) to capture as much of the launch as possible, though the situation would hardly be optimal. The other camera, the size of a pen, would be wired onto Ronny and hopefully would record the entire descent; that camera had an altimeter.

They would wait until dusk. They would dress in stealth clothing. They would cut the lights on the van and coast. They would memorize their alibis and they would remain calm.

"Questions," the Doctor addressed the kitchen.

Not a word about the wings. Vivian looked straight at Ronny and made her announcement.

"I'm coming," she said.

Then she looked from Ronny to the Doctor to Paul, making sure her message was clear, and left the room.

The day passed more quickly than one might expect of a day tasked solely with ending. The hours discarded without fanfare. Ronny split the time between trying to lounge on the couch and loitering out back, chain-smoking into the late afternoon. Vivian sequestered in the guest room, writing a letter to Seth. She folded his birth certificate into a crisp rectangle around the old snapshots of their grandparents and their mother, and sealed the envelope with masking tape. She copied the address from her postcard. C/O Las Vegas Regal Vistas, Seth Foster, Camp 215B, Filibuster Parkway E., Las Vegas, NV 89123.

Ronny knocked on the door at quarter past seven, the early winter evening already slaking through its third hour of dark. He wore a black shirt (with the back cut out, then stapled back together in hasty accommodation for the wings), dark corduroy pants, dark running shoes, black ski cap.

Vivian felt like crying at the sight of him, up close. He was stuck now, with this other body, and had the Doctor even thought of that? Of what happened after the flight, when Ronny was left in the world this way? How could he have let himself agree, and submit, to this? She tentatively drew her hand up to touch the wing's mantle, and her fingers dragged across the roughened skin. She was taken aback by how animal they were, and realized that all along she had been imagining disposable party wings that glittered and flung, bright white and iridescent, even though she'd known better.

"You don't have to do this," he said.

Her eyes caught the messy stapling that skirted his shoulder blades, tugging the jersey of his shirt into twisted pleats. "Does it hurt?" she said.

"It's a lot better. It's not that bad."

She tilted her mouth to his and kissed him, once, sadly. He was warm with recent sleep. She stepped back, pulled on her dark purple cutoff gloves, and folded the envelope in half, stuffing it in the back pocket of her jeans. She took his hand and they went downstairs, out to the waiting van.

The ride to the quarry was agonizing. The Doctor mumbled something about surveillance Vivian didn't catch, and kept his eyes glued to the rearview mirror as he drove. Ronny sat in the way-back, draped in a floral bed sheet. Paul sat shotgun and fooled with the light meter, trying to screw it into the neck of the collapsible tripod. Ronny stared out the window, his head pressing the cold glass, thinking how many times he had meant to skip town, leave it for good; that was top on the list of his enumerated failures, which, at this point, he should probably quit counting. Vivian pictured the trailer in the woods, not the way it had actually looked as she'd fled—smudge of ailing spruce or winter pock or, really, just the thinnest pollen of haze rising—but as a palette of aluminum kindling conducting electricity bold enough to rearrange the constellations.

The mist rolled at the edge of the quarry; rose up from its basalt mouth and dissipated. The Doctor examined the wings under the dim moonlight, refusing to turn on the flashlight Paul pulled from the van's glove box. His hand paused at the two-inch wide glider woven on the underside where he'd had to reapply resin earlier in the week when a thread of the polymer binding had split. The tear loosened a fraction of wing tip, which caused a narrow channel where the air flow would concentrate, which would, in turn, alter wind shear. Would determine whether the wings were capable of soaring.

Ronny wondered if the Doctor had any small misgivings, or could conceive that any part of the operation, having driven their contingency to the edge of a canyon, might be a mistake. How had Ronny gotten mixed up in it. Was his regular life really that bad, so he'd signed himself right up for whatever guinea pig assignment had offered some distraction? He bet he could reevaluate all his choices of the past three years and still end up right fucking there, where he was, sure, but he withheld a flimsy hope that he might've figured a way out. It didn't mean he wasn't going through with it. If there was any possible redemption for the mediocrity he had chosen, he would be a fool to walk away from it.

The Doctor and Paul were discussing where best to station the tripod: according to Ronny's position and how far forward they could expect him to jump, an imprecise angle. The Doctor stooped at the ground and unspooled a tape measure while Paul marked off the paces, scuffing at the dirt with the heel of his boot.

Vivian had been pacing, trying to keep warm and trying to walk off some of her nervous energy. Trying to keep out of the fray as the Doctor and Paul made educated guesses about trajectory and Ronny stretched in what looked like slow motion calisthenics, organizing and reorganizing his new weight. She was making her twenty-third round of the van when she heard the alarm cast out into the shapeless distance, an ember.

From across the field, off in the direction of the highway, a siren began building its slow wail into the night. It started as a howl muffled in the wind, then sharpened into a shrill keening. The sound was undeniable. By the time the blue strobe was cutting through the fog and growing larger, lobbing flashes wide, they all stood frozen with the recognition that they had been followed, had been found, and were on the brink of being caught.

Vivian was dumbfounded. They were trespassing, sure, but what was the big deal—there was a part of it that made no sense, though she was convinced that the Doctor was to blame. Or Paul. Why weren't they jumping in the van, why weren't they taking off before they got arrested, what were they *doing* just standing there like that, just frozen in place while they could be running or driving—

The Doctor had started up in German, a manic, desperate rant no one seemed to understand. Ronny walked over to Vivian, who stood clasping her hands so tight her knuckles turned white in her fingerless gloves, and pressed his lips to her forehead.

"No," she said as he started to back away, grabbing his sleeve, her voice breaking before it could make it past her throat. Everything was ending. She felt dizzy. The Doctor was shouting and half-crying; Paul cursed at his camera and thumped the tripod to the ground so hard it cracked.

Ronny moved toward the quarry and Vivian moved with him, the sirens so loud, by then the cops were less than a third of a mile away, they were half a mile, they were a parking lot's distance, the strobes of light scattered and refracted endlessly through the fog, and Ronny took another step.

Vivian had him by his sleeve and he tried to shake her off. Just as the gravel started to spin under the police vehicle's tires, skidding up to the van, Ronny said, "Vivian, I have to go. Come on, get—" he shoved her a little, "—out of here, go."

In a flash of desperation, she jumped at Ronny, grabbed at his neck and shoulders, wrapping her ankle around his knees; she threw herself at him and clung to his side. She threw herself at him, and they stumbled in awkward collision to the edge, over the edge, were already falling as the cop shouted through his bullhorn, "Nobody move."

Ronny and Vivian fell, swung heavy and faltering over the canyon. They plummeted, lumbering to remain barely entwined. Vivian's scream caught in her throat. It was too hard to breathe. Blood pounded in her ears, pounded behind her eyes, pounded her lungs, pounded her chest in a deafening, raging panic. Adrenaline: her heart shattered. Her face stung, her eyes stung, whipped by the wind slicing past them as they sank into another darkness.

Each time the wings lifted, swept up on a strong current, it seemed briefly as if they would fly after all—steadied aloft and suspended for half a second—then the gust waned, dropping them abruptly. It happened four times, and every time they hurtled deeper into the gaping expanse.

Vivian felt her grip loosen, felt her body slacken and start to slip from Ronny's, his waist slipping, his thighs slipping, his knees. They fell faster. And it grew colder. And it grew relentlessly silent.

And the sky that had floated above them, the expanse of their inverse, disappeared. A low-slung fog obscured the opening of the quarry, where they had stood just a moment earlier. Where the Doctor had knelt in grief. Where the cop had reached authoritative fingers to his holster. Where Paul had fumbled with the camera in the dirt. Where Ronny and Vivian had rolled over the roughly hewn lip of earth and into the stretch of black that went on and on.

Vivian let go. And everything continued to darken in retreat. Ronny seemed to rise farther from her, lifting quickly upward until suddenly she could no longer make out his peculiar man-bird shape. She didn't think of anything in particular, nothing remarkable. No faces flashed before her eyes. No madrigal voices rose in choir, and she had no revelations. Nothing. Nothing. Nothing happened and nothing happened and nothing happened until everything had fallen away, until it was over too quickly and there was nothing left, nothing, no derivative of silence, no bones stitched from wind and wing.

Somewhere out there, in the middle of a dying field, someone struck a match to spark. The field was aglow. The field was ablaze.

After everything, there could be only one possible outcome. Things turned out the only way they could. And maybe a part of him had known how the odds were stacked back then, before everything that happened, but he definitely knew it now, as the summer died off around him and he was left to endure his strange new anatomy without the stares of the crowd to bolster him. The feeling that he was special didn't last even the short time it took the voyeurs to shuffle to the next tent over with their meaty hands and their dollar bills. And the brutal weight of the wings in the heat and humidity quickly took a toll on his body, imposed a permanent slumping posture on his narrow shoulders. His whole new body ached.

Ronny finished off his beer, pitched the can at the nearest truck parked across the field, and fished another out of the cooler. The winter and spring had been a blur of chaotic time passing, but the muggy south Georgia summer dragged unbearably out before him, around him, after him. There were many afternoons, circling the main cage, when he didn't think he'd make it through another hour, let alone another day. The depressing thing was that he had made it through. Had almost made it through the entire season, minus the two weeks that remained.

Ronny heard footsteps behind him in the gravel, felt the picnic table creak lower as the Doctor sat down next to him. Ronny nodded to the cooler. They didn't say anything for awhile, and then Ronny broke the silence.

"Where to, after this?" he said, for something to say; he was of no real opinion on the move. He only had two geographies: before the quarry and after the quarry.

The Doctor shook his head, took a long swallow from his can. "I heard the new trainers talking about Calexico, I think, that or Baton Rouge."

Ronny nodded. They'd resigned themselves to being partners, Ronny and the Doctor, though it was still sometimes difficult to feel like allies. But they were stranded here in this new life together, Mad Doctor and Bird Man, stuck perpetuating the vision, even after it had failed. Except it hadn't failed, though, had it, since Ronny's wings actually worked, much to their boss's delight: people lined up early and by the dozens to see Ronny the Bird Man fly simple figure eights around the rafters of the main tent.

And Ronny couldn't go on hating the Doctor for the risk he himself had taken. He hated himself too much for what had happened to Vivian to have any hate left over for anyone else. Almost nine months had passed, and he still couldn't sleep through the night. He figured he was bound to eventually run into Seth on the circuit, and he dreaded that inevitability. But maybe, with any luck, Ronny would be long gone by then. He was saving all the cash they paid him every week, so that he could quit this life, finish out his days in the woods of the Blue Ridge or somewhere, as far away from all this as he could manage. He wondered what the Doctor's escape plan was. They didn't discuss such things.

Ronny stood, pitched the empty can he was holding at the same truck, and said, "Well, I think I'm going to turn in, Doc."

As he walked away, the Doctor called out to him. "Let's practice that new glide technique tomorrow, Ron, I think it'd be great for the finale."

Ronny didn't answer, already out of earshot and not listening anyway; he was too far gone.

In his cabin, he closed his eyes and tried to get comfortable on his stomach, the only way he could sleep anymore, the only way he'd ever be able to sleep. It wasn't easy to relax. The wings pressed down on him as they flattened out over his body, heavy like a section of scaffolding from a bridge. His body felt like a tin can crushed beneath them. He hoped the alcohol would obscure some of the visions that plagued the long hours, without fail, each night. He'd gone to see his father once before he died, after all the media attention had died down, and he still couldn't get that visit out of his head, his father slumped under a bundle of quilts but still shivering, eyesight gone, his mouth slack, his body lean and sunken. Ronny had leaned over the bedside to hug his father, and his father had reached out to him, but when he touched the edge of the wing, he'd withdrawn his arm, horrified, instantly. Ronny knew his father couldn't see him, to understand, but the way he'd been too disgusted to even touch him—it kept him up on the rare night when thoughts of Vivian didn't.

He gave up trying to drift off. He pulled the box out from under his bed and halfheartedly prepared the dose. The syringe plunged ice cold into his skin: four sunsets' distance to the clearing. Two more weeks to get through, he thought. Two more weeks. He got back into bed and waited for the dark to dissolve the world around him, turn it into something brighter, something more bearable, with a different ending.

Allison Titus is the author of the chapbook *Instructions from the Narwhal* (Bateau Press, 2007) and the book of poems *Sum of Every Lost Ship* (Cleveland State University Press, 2010). She is the recipient of a fellowship from the National Endowment for the Arts.

Books from Etruscan Press

Etruscan Press Is Proud of Support Received From

Wilkes University

Youngstown State University

The Raymond John Wean Foundation

The Ohio Arts Council

The Stephen & Jeryl Oristaglio Foundation

The Nathalie & James Andrews Foundation

The National Endowment for the Arts

The Ruth H. Beecher Foundation

The Bates-Manzano Fund

The New Mexico Community Foundation

Drs. Barbara Brothers & Gratia Murphy Fund

Founded in 2001 with a generous grant from the Oristaglio Foundation, Etruscan Press is a nonprofit cooperative of poets and writers working to produce and promote books that nurture the dialogue among genres, achieve a distinctive voice, and reshape the literary and cultural histories of which we are a part.

etruscan press
www.etruscanpress.org

Etruscan Press books may be ordered from

Consortium Book Sales and Distribution
800.283.3572
www.cbsd.com

Small Press Distribution
800.869.7553
www.spdbooks.org

Etruscan Press is a 501(c)(3) nonprofit organization.
Contributions to Etruscan Press are tax deductible
as allowed under applicable law.
For more information, a prospectus,
or to order one of our titles,
contact us at books@etruscanpress.org.